D0934759

BY

TEJU COLE

TREMOR

TREMOR

—

A NOVEL

—

TEJU COLE

RANDOM HOUSE

NEW YORK

Copyright © 2023 by Teju Cole

All rights reserved.

Published in the United States by Random House,
an imprint and division of Penguin Random House LLC, New York.

RANDOM HOUSE and the HOUSE colophon are
registered trademarks of Penguin Random House LLC.

LIBRARY OF CONGRESS CATALOGING-IN-PUBLICATION DATA
NAMES: Cole, Teju, author.
TITLE: Tremor: a novel / Teju Cole.
DESCRIPTION: First Edition. | New York: Random House, [2023]
IDENTIFIERS: LCCN 2022056649 (print) | LCCN 2022056650 (ebook) |
ISBN 9780812997118 (Hardback) | ISBN 9780812997125 (Ebook)
CLASSIFICATION: LCC PR9387.9.C67 T74 2023 (print) |
LCC PR9387.9.C67 (ebook) | DDC 823/.92—dc23/20111128
LC record available at https://lccn.loc.gov/2022056649
LC ebook record available at https://lccn.loc.gov/2022056650

Printed in Canada on acid-free paper

randomhousebooks.com

4 6 8 9 7 5 3

Book design by Barbara M. Bachman

TREMOR

ONE

THE LEAVES ARE GLOSSY AND DARK AND FROM THE DYING blooms rises a fragrance that might be jasmine. He sets up the tripod and begins to focus the camera. He has pressed the shutter twice when an aggressive voice calls out from the house on the right. This isn't the first time this kind of thing has happened to him but still he is startled. He takes on a friendly tone and says he is an artist, just photographing a hedge. You can't do that here, the voice says, this is private property. The muscles of his back are tense. He folds the tripod, stows the camera in its bag, and walks away.

ON MONDAY HE GOES to the department where packages and other mail await him, among them a white envelope with a quarter-inch-thick black line along its flap. Two or three envelopes of this kind arrive each month, official announcements of the passing of past or current members of the faculty. The envelope is almost square. He sits in his office and opens it. The card inside is also trimmed in black. An emeritus professor of microbiology, not someone he knows, has died. The cards don't deviate from a formula: the dean expresses regret at the death of the professor in question in antiquated language. A death that "occurred on the sixth instant" is one that happened on the sixth of this month; "the fifteenth ultimo" is the fifteenth of last month. He has begun to collect the cards, thinking of them in their high-toned formality as an echo of the mourning dress worn in previous times, the silks and grenadines of widows' gowns in the Civil War era, the black veils, black gloves, and black jewelry that let society know a grief was being observed. That symbolic order of colors is gone now, that tracking of heavy, full, or partial mourning in the language of black, gray, purple, lavender.

There are two books on his desk: Calvino's *Invisible Cities* and a translation of the *Epic of Sundiata*. The latter contains versions of the epic by two different djeli, Bamba Suso and Banna Kanute, and he has recently finished reading Bamba Suso's version. On one of the bookcases is a bottle of dark ink sent to him by Paul Lanier. The ink is made from wild grapes collected around railway tracks in St. Louis and because it is homemade, the color has shifted. In the bottle it still looks deep, close to violet, but brushed on paper it has now taken on a pale color reminiscent of the sea. But "the sea" how? When we say the sea is blue we are thinking of a light or pale blue, a color close to sky blue. The sea is sometimes one of those blues and sometimes a darker version of them but the sea is also often not blue at all: it is sometimes orange, sometimes gray, sometimes purple with the iridescence of Homer's πορφύρεος, sometimes nothing, transparent, water. At dusk it goes from silvery to pewter. On a moonless night it is black.

He picks up the bottle of ink, an aged lavender, a purple haunted in its lower registers by indigo. The African violet is where the name comes from but he also loves the false web of etymologies the name summons: the tenderness of a viol, the strain of a violin, the hint of violence. Not the violet of medieval bishops and university professors but rather the violet of darkest African skin. Paintings by Mark Rothko, Agnes Martin, Lorna Simpson, but above all Chris Ofili in the lower register of whose *Mary Magdalene* is a violet so deep it could drown the eyes, in whose *Raising of Lazarus* there is a violet so base it could raise the dead. The hand-dyed, hand-spun cloth that he took from his grandmother's wardrobe a few months after her death. Gray for loss, violet for love.

THEY GO UP TO Maine to shop for antiques. The trip takes an hour and a half and during the brief crossing into New Hampshire they switch places and she drives. The plan is to do a small stretch of southern Maine up to Kennebunk, visiting several shops. They have set aside the entire afternoon. At a large emporium in York he looks at a nineteenth-century map of North America hand-drawn by a child. On the outskirts of Ogunquit are yard signs saying "Blue Lives Matter" which in town give way to rainbow flags. Finally they come to Wells where they find a large shop set in a building that might once have been a barn. The shop, on two levels, is crammed with furniture, paintings, glassware, and porcelain, many of them from the early or mid-nineteenth century and quite a few older. They wander separately. She looks at a maple colonial-style drop-front desk. He is surprised to find a section with an assortment of wooden masks and sculptures, three of them recognizably African, the others possibly Pacific, Asian, or Native American. He is immediately drawn to an elegant antelope headdress with a soaring pair of horns, a ci wara. It stands around four feet tall and appears to be old, its wood stained dark, the information on the label imprecise.

The sinuous lines and open-work carving depict a female antelope with a baby antelope carved onto her back, the fawn a miniature of the mother, their main difference being that its horns are not as proportionally long. Ci wara, credited by Bambara people with having brought agriculture to humanity, is danced in its male and female forms as headdresses for young men during sowing and harvesting festivals.

The two men who run the antiques shop seem to be in their mid-to-late eighties and their banter has the feel of a long-practiced comedic act. They tell Tunde that they are brothers-in-law but frequently taken for brothers. One jokes about the other being too old, the other jokes about the other not being handsome enough to be related to him. Tunde asks the slightly younger-looking man about the ci wara but the man has little additional information beyond the notion that the sculpture "might be authentic."

To himself Tunde wonders what authenticity would mean. That this particular ci wara has been danced in a Bambara agricultural festival? Or that whether or not it was danced it was not made for the tourist trade, that it was made by Bambara people for the use of Bambara people? Whatever its story it had found its way to the coast of New England. It was in a shop among the unrelated treasures white people had collected by fair means or foul from across the globe. In the West a love of the "authentic" means that art collectors prefer their African objects to be alienated so that only what has been extracted from its context becomes real. Better that the artist not be named, better that the artist be long dead. The dispossession of the object's makers mystically confers monetary value to the object and the impor-

tance of the object is boosted by the story that can be told
about its role in the history of modern European art.

He has seen, in the past, a female ci wara figure compara-
ble to the one he is looking at now sold at auction for $400,000.
Those zeros, he knows, have everything to do with the trail of
magic words that the auction house brushed over the object:
"collected in situ," "acquired," "exhibited." The more extensive this account of ownership the greater the sums that can
change hands between sellers and buyers. The ci wara he is
looking at in Wells is priced at $250 which seems to settle the
question of authenticity: the sculpture has no "provenance"
and thus its value is minimal. He feels he ought to rescue it.
He wants to bring it closer to home, closer to his own home
where it can be seen by kinder eyes, by eyes that place authenticity elsewhere. Why should the labor of the contemporary
artist who makes a ci wara to sell to visitors be less deserving
of honor than that of the "traditional" artist who makes a ci
wara to be danced at a harvest festival? But he doesn't want to
fool himself. Money is still changing hands.

Sadako has decided that she wants the maple desk. It is
compact and likely to fit into the back of their rented SUV. At
the last minute he has doubts about the ci wara but Sadako
insists that they buy it. They go up to the front of the shop
where the rafter above the sellers is covered with photographs, cartoons, and clippings from old ads. Behind the
counter is a card signed by Laura Bush. This does not surprise him as the Bush family compound is only fifteen minutes away in Kennebunkport and this part of Maine is a
venerated area for the genteel wing of the political right. On
a wooden post near the counter, among the faded flyers and

curling laminated notices, he sees a small photocopied note in all-caps, worn by time and undated:

WELLS HOMESTEAD. THIS HOMESTEAD WAS SETTLED IN 1657 BY DR. THOMAS WELLS. IN AUGUST OF 1703 HIS GRANDSON DEACON THOMAS WAS AWAY LOOKING FOR A NURSE FOR HIS WIFE SARAH (BROWNE) WHO HAD GIVEN BIRTH THE EVENING BEFORE TO A DAUGHTER. WHILE HE WAS AWAY THE TOWN OF WELLS WAS ATTACKED BY INDI-ANS. THEY STRUCK AT THIS FARM FIRST. AXING THEIR WAY INTO THE HOUSE, THEY MASSACRED MRS. WELLS, HER IN-FANT, 4 YEAR OLD SARAH AND 2 YEAR OLD JOSHUA. THEN THEY BURNED THE HOUSE DOWN. AFTER THIS TERRIBLE TRAGEDY MR. WELLS LEFT FOR IPSWICH, MASSACHUSETTS, RETURNING SOMETIME AFTER 1718 WITH A NEW FAMILY TO RECLAIM THE HOMESTEAD. IT REMAINED IN THE WELLS FAMILY UNTIL 1906.

The older of the brothers-in-law rings them up. He tries to figure out the sales tax on a calculator with large buttons and gets it wrong the first time. Slowly he repeats the calcula-tion and gets it wrong again, arriving at the correct figure only on his fourth attempt. The equipment in the shop is ru-dimentary, evidently by design. The card reader into which Tunde's credit card has been inserted beeps for a few mo-ments before letting out an even tone. The man writes out a receipt on thin yellow paper then the brothers-in-law wrap the ci wara in sheets of soft white paper. Their trembling liver-spotted hands seem to be caressing the sculpture, array-ing it in gossamer white robes for a bridal. The antelope horns poke through the soft paper. Thus dressed the ci wara feels light as air. Sadako carefully takes it out to the SUV. Tunde brings the three drawers of the maple desk outside, then the desk itself.

Wild geese cross overhead honking in the falling dusk. Sky and sound are one and across from the barn is a house with the obvious modern additions of a third floor and a screened-in porch. Between the house and the barn stands the great old tree under which their SUV is parked. All time is now.

THE HEADLIGHTS POOL AHEAD of them on I-95. "If You Don't Believe" by Deniece Williams is the music that fills the car. A favorite of Sadako's. Thinking about Wells he can feel something unknotting in his brain. After nearly three decades in the U.S. his sympathies have been tutored in certain directions. He learned early that a "terrible tragedy" meant the victims were white. Later and by bitter experience he came to understand that there is always more to tragedies than is narrated, that the narration is never neutral. But what is happening to him now is stranger: this lack of sympathy for the Wells family, the way he struggles even to imagine them. So great a counterreaction is a new, brutal tone in him. Is it brutal? All he can think about is that in the period of the so-called Third Indian War, Abenaki people were dispersed by the colonial settlers, dispersed by those who took it as their God-given right to seize their lands, who took it as their right to kill them if they resisted.

But the note in the antiques shop was a fever dream of mindless Indian violence against people like "us." Later

Tunde will find the names and birth dates of Deacon Wells's children in county records: Sarah Wells, March 9, 1699; Joshua Wells, October 9, 1701. The Indians were without names and they had come bearing axes and they had killed and scalped and they had burned the place down. And yet Deacon Wells had returned fifteen years later with his losses restituted to him as Job's were, bringing with him a new wife, a cousin from Salem who had borne him three children. In time the land was pacified. The Indian problem went away and Deacon Wells lived long, until August 1737 when he committed his soul to the Lord. His will was proved the month after that. "I give and bequeath unto my dearly beloved wife Lydia Wells all my household stuff of every sort and kind, [and] my negro man Jeff."

THE FOLLOWING WEEKEND THEY have dinner with their friend Emily Brown at her home on Dana Street, a ten-minute stroll from their house on Ellis. A warm night, the feeling more late summer than early fall. At dinner he mentions the excursion to Wells. His recollection of the violent incidents at the homestead prompts Emily's partner Mariam to tell him about a book published in 2007 by Susan Faludi. *The Terror Dream*, Mariam says, connects the machismo of the Bush presidency to a long-running American obsession with captivity narratives, a tradition that began in colonial times and saw its main task as protecting white women from dark-skinned invaders. At home that night Tunde looks up the book and sees that there is a copy available at the library of the Kennedy School.

On Tuesday an hour before he is to teach his Digital

Color seminar he walks across the Yard through Harvard Square and down John F. Kennedy Street to the brick complex of the Kennedy School. In the library he dawdles. He has just settled down with a handful of magazines when one of the librarians hurries towards him. She wants to know if she can "help" him with anything. It is said in a tone he recognizes. Without a word, he walks away from her. He finds *The Terror Dream* and uses the self-checkout machine.

WHILE COOKING DINNER HE puts on the recording of Bach's Cello Suites he had bought on your advice sometime around 2001. In those days you were interested in the way Bach's written scores showed evidence of having originated in improvisation. You described it as "embodiment": the multifocal sensitivity an animal would have in a forest but also the alertness and contained intensity of a hunter in a different part of the same forest. Bach was not merely arranging notes, you said to Tunde at the time. He was conveying a living and intentional search, the presence of which could most deeply be felt in his solo works. A listener could follow this movement like a tracker, from one phrase to another, from one argument to another, a listener could inhabit this present tense no matter how festive or solemn the music got. And it was precisely the ability of the cellist Anner Bylsma to draw out these improvised-sounding lines that led you to recommend his recording to Tunde.

At the time of that correspondence Tunde had his own long-nurtured enthusiasm for recordings of Bach's solo works. He loved the debut on solo violin by Hilary Hahn, the Goldberg Variations played on piano by Chen Pi-hsien, and

narrator → you → Tunde

verve —

Jean-Pierre Rampal's performance of the partita for solo flute. In each of these recordings he found that quality of personal impersonality that made Bach feel less like a composer and more like a philosopher, a counselor, a scientist, an architect, or a prophet; anything but a regional court musician in eighteenth-century Germany.

Your recommendation of Bylsma, whom you described as having the verve of a fencer and the poise of a dancing master, had helped him experience this personal impersonality in a new way. It was almost, you said, as if Bylsma were making a drawing not playing a cello, so precise was his combination of light attack and ample sound. Tunde listened carefully to the recording back then and Bylsma's playing added much to his experience of works he already knew through several recordings.

The special value you saw in Bylsma's version and that you conveyed to Tunde was perhaps connected to your own practice in those days of composing free improvisations for piano, an approach that had less to do with the interpretation of preexisting works than with a spirit of discovery that invited the piano to reveal its secrets to you in real time. You said embodiment was not only the animal in the forest and the tracker following that animal but also the forest as a self-aware system, attentive to the rustle of its own leaves, the shifting colors, the air, the water, the panoptic view of many moving parts, the interactions of light and shade. Collective listening, you called it.

DURING THE MANY CONFLICTS between Native Americans and American settlers abductions were frequent, abductions that were later pressed into the service of a national myth. As many as a third of the hundreds of women who were kidnapped by Native Americans later refused to rejoin their white communities, finding that they preferred their new lives with their now adopted families. Meanwhile their white family members continued to believe that rescuing an abducted woman was the highest ideal no matter what the women themselves wanted. Hundreds of captivity narratives resulted and the ideal of heroic rescue deeply influenced American culture, not least in films like the 1956 John Wayne vehicle *The Searchers*.

The Searchers was a fictionalized account of the life of Cynthia Ann Parker who was taken by Comanche warriors in 1836 when she was ten. Parker lived with Comanche people for twenty-four years until she was brought back to her white family against her will. The story the film presents is one of pure heroism but in reality Parker, named Naduah by her Comanche family, had become a wife to a chieftain and a mother of three children and had spent ten years failing to reintegrate to white society. She tried to return to her Comanche family but was forcibly brought back a second time. Finally, following the loss of her daughter to pneumonia in 1871, she began to refuse food and slowly starved herself to death.

Long before that the brutality of the New England colonists had forced the Wampanoag chief Metacomet to go to war in defense of his people. Metacomet's Rebellion or King Philip's War as the colonists called it was costly for all the belligerents but especially devastating for the Native people of New England. In 1675 the colonists had burned alive six hundred Narragansett people, about half of them women and children, in Rhode Island. In March 1697 a band of Abenaki people responding to the French offer of bounties for British scalps attacked the village of Haverhill. They killed twenty-seven people and abducted thirteen. Among the abducted were Hannah Duston who had just had a baby and Mary Neff her midwife. Duston's week-old daughter Martha was immediately dashed against a rock by the attackers. Two weeks later and a hundred miles from home the two women were held by an Abenaki clan of twelve on Contoocook Island in the Merrimack River in what is now New Hampshire. Alongside them was Samuel Lennardson a British boy who had been captured eighteen months earlier.

TUNDE READS THIS CATALOG of horrors with a neutral spirit. He cannot decide now where his compassion is directed or whether his mood is as cold as it was in considering the Wells massacre. Perhaps it is Faludi's book that has fatigued him. No, not the book: it is history's own brutality, which refuses symmetries and seldom consoles. One night on Contoocook Island as the Abenaki family slept the white captives armed themselves with hatchets and went to work. Two of the Natives escaped, a woman and a boy. As for the others, Mary Neff killed one and Hannah Duston killed nine. Of those dead two were men, two women, and six children. Duston and Neff made their escape and had gone a little way already when, remembering a reward promised by the Massachusetts legislature, a reward for which evidence would be needed, Duston returned to the island and scalped all the dead. Carrying the grisly trophies she once again began the long journey home. She scalped them all. Their names are not known.

In the period that followed word of her exploits spread and she was positioned as an ambiguous hero. What she did was a strange thing for a woman to have done and the consensus that emerged is that she had demonstrated too much savagery. A legend requires clarity: who the enemy is, who the victim is, who the hero is. If that clarity is muddled all is lost. The Indians surely must be massacred, they surely must be scalped, but it is unwomanly work.

Faludi, citing the historian Mary Beth Norton, connects the idea of the Indian attack to the idea of the witch hunt. The girls who in that fateful final decade of the seventeenth century were bewitched or thought of as being bewitched in Salem, Massachusetts were often orphans who had lost one or both parents in the frontier wars. There was for instance Mercy Short who had been abducted from Salmon Falls, New Hampshire by Abenaki warriors in 1690. Both her parents and three of her siblings were among the thirty-four villagers killed during that raid. Freed eight months later through a ransom Short became a maid in Salem to a widow named Margaret Thacher. In 1692 after an errand to the Boston jail where some accused witches were being held, Mercy Short fell into fits. She had been "bewitched." But there can be little doubt her imagination was affected by her recent captivity and the horrors she had witnessed. Short gave a testimony to the fanatical Harvard-trained cleric Cotton Mather in which she said that she had seen the Devil. He was, she said, "a Short and a Black Man." But, she clarified, he was "not of a Negro, but of a Tawney, or an Indian color."

———

TUNDE IS STARTLED OUT of these thoughts by Sadako's return from work. They talk for a moment. She remains downstairs. He moves upstairs to her study. The room is lit by a single lamp and he continues reading. The conflict between the spirits of the invisible world and the people of New England had made Mather think "that this inexplicable War might have some of its Original among the Indians," who he believed had among them "horrid sorcerers, and hellish conjurers" who "conversed with Demons." A fear of the Indian invader most affected those towns on the outer reaches of the colonial settlements, the towns the colonists thought of as being in the border zone between order and disorder, Christianity and savagery, God and the Devil. The infamous witch hunts that convulsed the Salem Colony in 1692 and which swept along with them some twenty-four blameless souls, most of them women, most of them killed by hanging, had its beginnings in the false accusation made against Tituba, an enslaved woman likely of Taino or Carib origin who was described by her neighbors simply as "Indian." Under torture and after beatings Tituba confessed to being a witch. Because she confessed and because she was subsequently coerced into accusing others she was spared hanging. But the man who had enslaved her in Barbados, and in whose home she had lived in Salem, the Puritan minister Reverend Samuel Parris—he too had been trained at Harvard—now sold her off into a further and likely more brutal slavery. After that second sale Tituba, who had been forced to leave her toddler daughter in the Parris household, disappeared from the historical record. When Reverend Parris died twenty-eight years later in 1720 Tituba's daughter was bequeathed to his son Samuel Parris, Jr. and from that moment nothing further is known of the girl except for her name as written in the will of the old man: *Violet*.

TWO

MASAKO AND SEAN HAVE LEFT. SADAKO HAS GONE TO BED. The evenings are not yet cool enough for jackets and Tunde, with Rae on the rooftop deck, pours more whisky. Saturn and Jupiter are low tonight and the moon which was full three days ago is waning. He does not know the night sky well but he knows some names and can make good guesses: Sirius, Arcturus, the brighter planets. Behind him where the sky is darker the galaxy pulses and he remembers that there is an app he seldom uses on his phone. When he was twelve, he tells Rae, he used to stand outside their new home in Ojodu and look at the stars. The skies were clear back then, the house in a still-forested area at the city's edge. One night, he remembers, he was with Michael the houseboy. If Michael is alive now, if there were any way of finding him, he would be approaching fifty and this is hard to imagine. Back then Michael was a skinny hard-eyed boy with yellowish skin that seemed stretched over his skull. He worked in the house and didn't go to school, an unjust but not unusual arrangement. That night they were looking at the moon and Tunde had said that he found it amazing that men had gone there. Michael had laughed. No one had gone to the moon, he said, and he had laughed again. After Tunde tells Rae this story they tell him about growing up in Alabama and attending Space Camp. My problem was the opposite, Rae says. There was astronaut imagery everywhere. Space travel was so real that it lost its magic.

THE FOLLOWING MORNING THE shower is running hot. Just as he is about to step in he sees that the bath soap is out. He can't find a replacement in the bathroom cabinets, neither the lavender he likes nor the plain white soap Sadako prefers. He decides to use one of two special bars of soap he has been saving. He will use one and save the other forever. This is soap he bought at one of the galleries in Kassel where documenta 14 took place. The raw soap was stacked and packaged there and sold, each bar in a dark gray cardboard box and each box signed with the artist's name: Otobong Nkanga. Nkanga had said that the circuit of manufacture and distribution, the bringing into a gallery space of commerce, craft, installation, sculpture, performance, and activism, was integral to her idea of the art. The profits from selling the soap would be used to pursue art initiatives. A new foundation, an art space in her ancestral home of Akwa Ibom.

The ash of dried husks, plantain peels, or palm fronds: to this palm oil or shea butter is added, sometimes with herbs, and the combination is cured to create a soft black soap. Nkanga's soap developed from these traditional methods though in her case seven oils and butters sourced from Africa, the Middle East, and the Mediterranean were fused in a final stage with charcoal. Bathing with her soap now Tunde remembers how black soap, ose dudu, used to make him unhappy when he was little. He was a city kid and anything that didn't come in a printed package, anything that smelled like it was made in a village, put him off. Ose dudu was like àgbo, *paucity -*

the medicinal concoction of herbs people used for a variety of ailments. He found both vaguely embarrassing. He didn't see the need for black soap when there were perfectly good pharmaceutical brands like Joy and Imperial Leather. He had only ever used black soap at the insistence of his parents or grandparents and he came to associate its use with their insistence.

HE NOW TRIES TO remember. Did they move to Ojodu before Michael came to live with them? By the time he left for the U.S. five years later Michael was gone. The house back then was in a remote estate with a few scattered homes. The family's move from Ikeja had meant a new relationship with the city. Everything was suddenly farther away and there was a great deal more driving to do to get to school or church or to visit friends.

But he and the twins also had to contend with a changed terrain. A paucity of tarred roads meant bumpy journeys home from school, more time inside the huge clouds of red dust that filled the air of the city, dust that dirtied their clothes and bodies except for when the car was sealed shut and the air conditioner was on. But the air conditioner broke down often and he and his sisters ended up inhaling a lot of that dust. That turned out to be the lesser of their air pollution worries. Seven or eight minutes' walk away from home was a roadworks plant. The roadworks had three stacks which spewed out black smoke (a typically cruel irony of Lagos life: to live near a roadworks in an area with few good roads). The black smoke contained large quantities of grit which on settling left extensive residue. The atmosphere around the plant was barely breathable and the smoke traveled far, all across the neighborhood.

For the next five years the grit became part of his life. There was no question of moving elsewhere. This was the family home, the one his parents had built, tangible proof of their labors. The country was under a military dictatorship and the roadworks belonged to a multinational company. In a country that was full of decrees but essentially lawless, to whom would a complaint be directed? His family was helpless under the rule of that smoke which glinted gray in the sun like mica and settled darker when it came down on the washing on the line, smelling like burning tar or rubber, stinging their eyes and getting into their tea, insinuating its way past the mosquito netting onto every bed, descending on the tables, chairs, and sofas of the house. It was an irritation and, as the family later confirmed, a medical injury.

Among his strongest memories of those days is sitting at the window-facing desk in his bedroom. There would be a chemistry book open in front of him and an art book on his lap, the two books signaling the way that his attention was divided and would for a long time afterwards be divided between science and art. In the half hour it took him to complete a reading of those four open pages, the two on the desk and the two on his lap, all four would be darkened by the efflux of the smokestacks. Only later did he understand that the same fine layer of pollutant was coating the trachea and lungs of everyone in the household: his mother and father, his two younger sisters, their aunt, their grandmother, the houseboy. Tiny black roads of grit coursed through them all. Many years later after he moved away from home his father's cough got perilously worse. The family hid it from him. The diagnosis was sarcoidosis. It was thought at the time that his father would die but his lungs responded to steroid treatment and he lived. Some years after that the roadworks closed down and the air of the neighborhood regained some of its former clarity.

Tunde had left for the U.S. when he was seventeen, well before his father's illness. By this time he had a direct relationship to God through Christ, intense and already shot through with sexual guilt. Just before his departure the man they call Alagba came to the house to pray for his journey and Tunde was given black soap as spiritual preparation for the upcoming trip. He was told to go bathe with it. He refused. He had no time for this white-robed version of Christianity. Alagba's approach which was as Christian as it was indigenous was not what his parents believed either but for them it wasn't finally about belief. It was about accepting as part of life anything that could help them fight the spiritual battles they did believe to be everywhere. They couldn't understand their son's narrow view, his born-again rectitude, and he could not understand them and did not wish to. He refused to use Alagba's soap. His mother and father were incensed at his ingratitude. On such matters his parents were always in agreement. The incident with Alagba was followed by yelling from his father and then silence from his father and everyone else. The twins, three years younger than he was, were confused by the whole thing and tried to keep a low profile. The house was like a tomb in those last days before his departure from Nigeria.

THE WATER HAS SLIGHTLY cooled. Suds of black soap pool onto the white soap dish. Life changes us and what he wants now is this. The fragrance of Nkanga's soap is delicate and under the hot water he immerses himself in the paradoxical thought of a blackness that wicks filth away. The swirls on the soap and on the soap dish take on sudden infinite depth. The soap is marbled and mobile. He bathes in nebulae.

With Michael that night in Ojodu he'd known almost nothing of the sky. He knew the moon, the existence of stars, and he had a vague memory of Halley's Comet which he'd heard about on the news but not seen in 1986. But he had no sure ground in anything astronomical so that when Michael laughed, when Michael suggested that the idea was risible that human beings had entered a metal vessel and fired themselves to *that*—Michael had pointed—to that over there, the moon, Tunde had understood some of the doubt. Michael's skepticism hadn't changed his mind but he had seen how the idea of space travel couldn't be easily absorbed into a view of the world that hadn't been educated into it.

Now many years later he has the names of a few stars. The Big Dipper is easy to spot and sometimes he'll see something yellowish, almost red and he'll realize that it's Mars. It amazes him that "Mars" is a word he can correctly connect to an object in the night sky. More important he now has an expanded sense of astronomy, the extensive learning it contains, subtleties inside of which Emily has spent her adult life. It is like knowing of the existence of a language he cannot yet speak but to which he is acoustically attuned.

A language has words and non-lexical phonemes and is not neatly split between perfectly fluent speakers and perfectly ignorant non-speakers. That kind of knowledge is a scale and somewhere on that scale is an awareness of unapprehended complexity, the knowledge that there is much that one does not know. There would have been no way to tell Michael all this, to tell him that the moon is real and space travel is real and doubt is real as well; not that Tunde had at the time more than an unsteady intuition of all of it himself.

HE CAN SENSE HER wakefulness. In the dark each waits for the other to sleep. Seventeen years together, fifteen years married. It is not that they are pretending to be asleep. The effort to fall asleep if someone else is in the room is indistinguishable from pretending to sleep. One performs sleep until sleep comes. Sadako's breathing soon changes and he knows now that she's asleep. Language: he imagines someone who knows little to no Yoruba at all but who knows how it sounds, how it moves in the air. This is part of what he likes about being in a university, where there is otherwise much to dislike, where the narrow valorization of disciplines can feel like a disciplining of his spirit. He likes that there are people at the university who have stared into the immense complexity of the Andromeda galaxy or of C. elegans or Sanskrit or geometry and have made it communicate with the immense complexity of their own brains. And this is one of the reasons he enjoys talking to Emily. Even when he struggles to understand the technical details of her work, which is almost always, there is a more-ness there he loves. He does not value expertise per se, as usually understood, but something related to it: the superlative in all places and in all cultures, that thing that is there in contemporary technologies and also there in traditional practices, that face of determined competence with which human beings confront a hostile universe.

In a talk in Naples last summer during the opening of *Tree of Heaven* someone asked him whom he most admired. When he finds himself onstage and is asked a broad question of this kind he tries to be game. He'll give an answer because he feels the point is not to deliver an incontrovertible response but to offer a reasonable possibility, to return serve. In Naples his response to the question of whom he most admired was "Pius Mau Piailug," a name that was met with the uncomprehending silence he had expected.

Pius Mau Piailug died in July 2010 at the age of seventy-eight. He was Micronesian and one of the few custodians, perhaps the only one, of an area of ancient knowledge: the art of navigating across vast waters without the aid of modern instruments. He sailed alone in a wooden boat in 1976 from Hawaii to Tahiti guided only by the knowledge he carried in his head and by what nature presented of itself to him: the movements of the stars by night, the position of the sun by day, the behavior of oceangoing birds, the color of the water and of the undersides of clouds, the taste of fish, the swelling of the waves. Who is to say the universe is hostile? All this information gathered up by the alert navigator and subtly interpreted made the ocean a friendly and readable book. He could tell when he was near an island or archipelago, when the water was fresher or saltier, when a storm was in the offing. For Mau the world was far more comprehensible than most people would ever know. People like him show that a deeper intimacy with nature is possible and that this intimacy does not have to rely on the obliterative arrogance of Western culture.

Tunde tells the audience it does him good to admire this man. Mau reminds him that life elsewhere is not only abundant but often more deeply abundant. He already feels this, particularly when he thinks about Yoruba culture or about the music he cherishes so much that at certain moments it strikes him as the "meaning" of life itself. The boastfulness of the Enlightenment and its liberal inheritors is a waste of time. But the life of Mau suggests one other thing, he'd said to the Naples audience: it suggests that profound traditional knowledge can sustain a human being in the moments of deepest solitude. Mau's journeys lasted a long time. The one from Hawaii to Tahiti took a month. That extended isolation, as much as the intricate know-how of ocean navigation, brings one into hushed amazement. The way we live now, Tunde said, the ability to go an entire month without any kind of human communication, would be seen as requiring almost superhuman fortitude. It would be a feat of endurance from a different era, an instance of physical as well as psychological self-reliance that is hard to imagine these days. Most of those who have to endure solitary confinement do not choose it.

Tunde is not conscious of having any particular interest in marine navigation or perilous adventure. And yet when he thinks about Mau he wants to change his own life. His first encounter with Mau was in the form of a written obituary. Since then he has read nothing else and hasn't been interested in doing so. His admiration for Mau is a chart he constructed from the clues in that single obituary, the memory of which fills him with the simple wish to be more in tune with the equivalents in his own life of the rising and falling of the waves, the flights of birds, the smell of the air. He wants to take in what is useful from the world not in order to plunder it but in order to live. He wants to move his boat with intention toward some purpose. He was able to convey only a fraction of this thinking to the audience in Naples. Possibly he had been too enthusiastic about what to them must have been arcane and unrelatable. Now the night is deep. He has drifted into that region in which conscious thoughts lap against the hull of dreams. He's still trying to fall asleep. Finally the trying is sleep.

IN THE MORNING SADAKO is gone. The parking spot in front of the house is as bare as it would be on any weekday but the difference is that this evening the car won't return. The spot will remain bare and will be bare for a few days. He has no use for the car and since there is parking at Masako's condo Sadako has driven herself there. She will keep the car while she's away. When he comes downstairs there's coffee in the French press. She's the early riser and always makes two cups. Had she made an exception today he would have been tempted to read more anger into her departure than is true. Who knows what's happening in someone else's head? He cannot with any confidence say what's happening in his own head.

Some obscure but persistent recent sourness between them is what has led to this brief separation. There have been many times in their life together when they have woken up intertwined and have lived in the mood created by that intimacy for the entirety of the day. There are many other times when each has kept to his or her own side of the bed. This departure is only a slight extension of that: a need to sleep in different houses. But the need is hers.

His heart aches. After all she is his wife and he is her husband. No they don't like the terminology but they have been fine with adopting it for the sake of their families for whom other terms wouldn't make sense. His heart aches but it is nothing like the deeper heartache of eight or nine years ago when their love was ruled by her fear of losing her freedom and his fear of abandonment, fears that colored all their disagreements back then and almost pushed them into a self-fulfilling prophecy of divorce. They survived those bad months (bad years, really) with a therapist's help. In the therapist's uninterrupting presence they heard again as though for the first time the things that they had said to each other in the heat of conflict. Through his help or through the fact of his having been in the room they had found their way back to each other and the contrasting fears had been quelled. But no feeling is final. They love each other but new mysteries germinate. He knows this without knowing what the current cloud is and if she knows what it is she has not or cannot yet put it into language.

He remembers advice he gave Kehinde two years ago when things were hard for her and Tomi: to own up to her part in it. Like so much advice it was easier given than acted on. What is his own part in this now? Tenderness, consideration, to try to see Sadako as she sees herself? The credible and winsome words assemble themselves in his mind but there's the stubborn gap between what he is able to think and what he is able to do.

THREE

———

HE BEGINS THE WORKSHOP BY ASKING THE STUDENTS WHAT has been preoccupying them lately. He wants them to enjoy each other's range and to examine their own experiences in the light of their classmates' reactions. Anything may be discussed during this opening segment of class, with the sole exception of Brexit. He intends for this to be taken as a joke but he finds that each time he says it he means it not entirely as a joke. An anticolonial side of him resents having to hear about British politics at all. Wasn't that the headache of being under the British Empire: being made to care about British customs, British history, British needs? His classroom ban seems to amuse some of his students though he can't be sure some of them do not also find it grating. After all no one likes being told what they can or cannot speak about. This term he has two British students. Fiona is taking his seminar and Anouk is working on a joint visual arts and astronomy thesis directed both by him and by Emily Brown. What do they think about his Brexit ban? Perhaps he is only being tolerated.

Last weekend Deborah watched *Ad Astra* which was in her view well produced but thinly plotted. It leads the class to discuss other recent big-budget space films like *Interstellar* and *Gravity*. What she most remembers of *Ad Astra*, Deborah says, is its soundtrack, which she has listened to several times since. Marcel and Meg are both "obsessed" with the new Lana

Del Rey album. Amina says she has been watching a series of videos posted by the FBI to YouTube in which a man named Samuel Little is interviewed by a Texas Ranger. Little, who was imprisoned in 2014 on a drug charge, was later found through DNA evidence to have been responsible for the murders of three women in California in the late 1980s. Javier is worried about the flooding in Spain where his parents and grandparents live. Tom is directing a theatrical production of *Death and the King's Horseman*. Eugene is in an acting class in which each student has been assigned to study a classmate with the aim of being "in character" as that classmate at the end of term. The assignations are anonymous: Eugene does not know which classmate is studying him and the classmate he's studying doesn't know that they're being studied.

AMINA, WHO MENTIONED THE Little case, is a research fellow auditing the workshop. Tunde returns to her and asks her to say more. Little's story emerged in bits, she tells the class. In 2018, in order to gain a concession, specifically in order to have his prison location changed from Los Angeles to the relative calm of a small facility in Texas, he began to confess to other crimes. Because of the credible details he presented Little was able to convince authorities that he was responsible for dozens of hitherto unsolved murders. The crimes stretched over a thirty-five-year period and almost all the victims were women. No fewer than ninety-three women died at his hands: quite literally at his hands, as strangulation was his preferred method. He is believed to be the most prolific serial killer in American history. The students are aghast. Why would they not have heard of this monster?

Tunde suggests to the class that they watch one of the interview clips Amina has discussed. Amina helps him to locate one under three minutes in length and he projects it from his laptop. When it begins to play he is surprised to see that Little is black and elderly and has a sweet manner. The most prolific American serial killer is black? The man is not wild-eyed like Charles Manson. And though he is evidently intelligent he does not seem to have the hostile insinuating charm of a Ted Bundy or Hannibal Lecter. Tunde is aware of the affective pressure of the word "elderly," a word he can hardly separate from tender and even protective feelings. Little's face and his mien, his small twinkling eyes, his merry raconteurish manner, all of it is familiar to Tunde from numerous experiences of hearing elders talk about long-ago events. But the story Little is telling is a story of extraordinary violence, a story of suffering meted out to others. Tunde doesn't know anyone who was murdered and when he hears about a murderer's victims he can only try to imagine what it means for those people's families.

IN THE CLIP AMINA has selected Little is the only figure on camera. He wears a light gray woolen cap, a white undershirt, and a wide-necked light blue prison shift which looks almost like a painter's smock. The video is so simple and effective that Tunde suspects that Amina, who is an alert student of photography, is drawn to it in part for its style. The Texas Ranger just offscreen asks Little about a girl who died around 1992 near Little Rock. "Oh I loved her," Little says with a quick smile and a hint of a Southern accent as though he really were recalling a sweet affair. He thinks her name was Ruth. She was heavyset with fair skin, and a gap between her teeth. He doesn't convey these details automatically. Sometimes his eyes take on a far-off look as though in the effort to accurately remember what he's about to say. The Ranger who is questioning him doesn't press hard and is in fact friendly, perhaps in order to get Little to keep talking.

Little says he picked Ruth up from a crack house and was with her for two or three days. They went shoplifting together at Sears and at Kroger. All this is recounted in a light tone though not mockingly, not as though to prepare us for the coming twist. He recounts it with what a casual listener might call genuine affection. At Kroger he's arrested for shoplifting but Ruth is not. For days after, she remains in the car and won't leave the store's parking lot, presumably pining for him, and it is for her sake that he's eventually released without charges. Together they head out of Little Rock towards Bentonville. There's an elision at this point in his narration. He says nothing of rape, nothing of murder, but instead begins to describe turning off the highway towards a cornfield beyond which is a pile of discarded cornstalks and, farther, the woods. He tells the Ranger how ten miles outside North Little Rock he drags Ruth's body—she is too heavy for him to carry, he says—to the cornstalks and lays it there, lays *her* there, with his car parked facing the highway.

The video ends and the class begins to discuss what they've just seen. While talking to the students Tunde suddenly fears he might break into sobs. The answer to the earlier question about why Little is not better known is right there: his victims were mostly black women, many of them sex workers, many of them addicted to drugs or in some way existing in the margins of society. If he sobs it will be because he wishes not to have watched this degradation in the company of students towards whom he feels a duty of care. And he particularly wishes not to have watched it with the two black women in the class—even though Amina who introduced the subject is herself one of those two—as though the knowledge of such things is something he should or could protect them from.

Samuel Little knew how to seek out victims whose deaths would not draw much attention. In other words he understood racism and misogyny and used that understanding as a cloak. Some of the killings had been declared unsolved and no great effort had been made to solve them. Others were ruled suicides or accidental overdoses likely because law enforcement could not be bothered to verify otherwise. This seventy-nine-year-old man telling stories of times gone by, occasionally smiling in his reverie, is a horrible human being by any ordinary measure and yet to him this was life. The meaning of his life was to find vulnerable women to destroy. A pure hatred of women, indistinguishable to him from love, was his sole reason for having come to earth.

THE CLASS NOW TURNS to the day's planned lesson. Two students are presenting Instagram-based photography projects. But Tunde's mind remains on Little. The way Little says with a smile, "I loved her." The way in his mind he had indeed loved Ruth for those three days before he violated and killed her, killed her because something in him told him he had to kill, killed her as he had killed and would kill others in eighteen other states beginning as far back as 1970, a patient and single-minded compulsion to extinguish life. Not only is he not remorseful, remorse does not occur to him as a possible response to something he finds so natural. But Samuel Little is not an abstract philosophical problem. He is a living man. The number of women he killed and thus the number of griefs he created short-circuits any attempt to "understand" the crime. All that the story teaches is that human suffering is a useless mystery.

AFTER CLASS TUNDE RECEIVES two emails. One is from an anonymous email account. It's not the first time. The message accuses him of being a fraud and being in a position that should have gone to someone more deserving. The other is from Hana confirming the talk at the Museum of Fine Arts. He responds with thanks and asks her to process the paperwork. Already he feels he might push them at this talk. He doesn't want to be rewarded for his ease or eloquence, he does not want to merely decorate the stage with his presence. How much innocence is a large institution like the museum due? But if he pushes too much that would be the behavior of a bad guest and might be taken as grandstanding. He is not worried about the price to be paid for talking about things people don't want to hear—the price might be ever-fewer invitations—but being misread as a cynic worries him. However free he might be he is not free of the desire not to be thought of as arrogant. But he still has some weeks to think this through. First will be the Santiago trip, which he is beginning to prepare for. He is to lecture about Lagos: a reality of his life so large and at the same time so intimate, intense, and various that he doesn't even know how to begin. The approach would have to be oblique.

He walks home under a cloudy sky. The afternoon has been gray and the sunset will be gray too. He's restraining himself from texting Sadako just yet and he likely won't do so tomorrow either. But the day after that he will text. She might delay responding. But he knows her, he knows she will be grateful to have been given the space and happy to have heard from him. From there, he hopes, they'll repair what needs repairing.

HE IS HOME. THE SKY is darkening more rapidly now and has taken on a stormy look. The curtains are open and he has not switched on the house lights. The sky reminds him of a sky from almost two decades before similarly roiled and gray as a sea. He was with Sandro on a ferry returning to Maui from Molokai. They were standing on the deck. The sky had only been intermittently clear that day, a weak blue and then the color of nothing. In the morning they'd gone for a hike from their overnight beach cabin. Sandro had loved the enormous landscape and the many hues of green but it had been ruined for him because though it was only raining lightly Tunde had brought an umbrella. Sandro was annoyed with Tunde for fussing with the umbrella and his annoyance had angered Tunde who did not see what was wrong with an umbrella. For Sandro this was proof that Tunde had no feeling for nature. They had spent the rest of the day with gritted teeth. The sky darkened over the sea and ferry and pulled Tunde's mood down with it.

Molokai was a leper colony once. Later the island had undergone forced development. The damned umbrella would have to be replaced. His mind was all over the place. He was thinking of music, "The Promise" by Tracy Chapman. Anything to still the violence beating in his heart. Why couldn't Sandro be better at loving him, why couldn't he get into his head how much Tunde loved him? There was an awkwardness, they were resolving it: Sandro was the more "out" of the two of them. But now it was clear that what love Sandro had for him was slipping away. Tunde was ashamed to be failing.

A heavy rain finally began and the horizon vanished in a haze. Everyone hurried off the deck of the ferry into the interior. The passengers were huddled and at the storm's mercy as the ferry was tossed on the swells. The squall lasted some twenty minutes and for that length of time he could not bear to look at Sandro. Instead he hummed "The Promise" over and over again letting sentiment sweep over him. When the ferry docked at Lahaina Harbor about forty-five minutes later Sandro turned to him and said he could no longer be with Tunde. What he said actually was that Tunde could no longer be with him. Whether this was an intentional distinction on his part or a slight mistranslation from the Italian in his head was hard to say for sure. What did it matter?

They took a taxi back to the rental in cold silence, damp clothes, and shared misery. At the rental they moved about avoiding each other. Tunde switched on a light in the living room and was suddenly thrown by a powerful electric shock. He collapsed to the tiled floor. Sandro rushed over to him frightened and Tunde pushed him away, barely able to do so, trembling and weeping like a broken child. A short while later he took a shower, still weeping. He had felt Death brush its fingers lightly across his face in this place far from anywhere he had ever called home. How would his parents have been told? When he came out of the shower, when he had dried himself and was warm and soothed, he found his way to his man's body on the mattress on the floor and was drawn in. The world became small and bearable again. Afterwards they fell asleep.

A YEAR LATER IT was over for real and three years after that, in 2004, Sandro was a distant memory. That summer Tunde visited Osaka with Sadako. They were walking around the city and she pointed to the hostel in Umeda where she had stayed in 1995 as a visiting student. She told him about how she had gotten up at five one morning as usual in preparation for a swim at the nearby Ogimachi pool. She liked to swim in the mornings before her classes, she loved being in the brightly lit pool and then coming back into the world at first light, walking in the just awakened streets of the unfamiliar city. She had gotten dressed that morning and was about to leave the apartment when everything started shaking. There was a full half minute of rattling. A bookcase in her room toppled over but she was in no greater danger than that. Only later would the full extent of the horror in Kobe be known, the utter shredding of infrastructure, the thousands dead. Osaka had been spared. When she told him about this, about how close she had been to it, there was quiet wonder in her voice and Tunde felt a retrospective shudder of fear on her behalf. But she had survived and nearly a decade had passed and they were there together on what was now a fine summer's day. The world felt good at that moment, full of a simple happiness no less wide and no less deep than sorrow. He held her in an embrace. We worry about close calls for the ones we love including the close calls they had long before we even knew they existed.

THE SKY IS FULLY DARK. He is careful as he switches on the lamp in the living room. Before he can talk himself out of it he navigates back to the FBI's YouTube channel and watches another video of Samuel Little and then another and another. The videos are all under four minutes, each edited from a longer interview. He notices in almost every case that the description of the actual moment of the woman's death is omitted. It cannot be that Little refuses to talk about those moments. The killing surely must be for him the narrative peak of each story. It is more likely that out of respect either for the victims or for the sensibilities of the public the narrative has been redacted. Still, in video after video, without reference to notes Little speaks of small towns and big cities and the poor neighborhoods in them that he used as his hunting grounds. He remembers the cars he owned or rented or stole, their make and model, their color and year, a Pontiac LeMans, a '78 El Dorado, a Lincoln Continental Mark III. He speaks about years and places, identifies streets and intersections by name, describes the road out of town, the vegetation, the usually isolated locations where he disposed of bodies, the woods, the bushes, the slopes, 1972 in Miami, 1984 in Columbus, 1993 in Las Vegas, 1982 in New Orleans. And he remembers above all the women themselves, their names, their faces, how tall they were, how much they weighed, he remembers them all with an unnerving softness. The woman in Miami is "transgender," Little says, and the Ranger cuts in to clarify that it is "a black male dressed up as a female." A white girl is a "dishwater blonde." Another black girl has "honey-colored skin." The woman in New Orleans has "a beautiful shape" and is "well put together." Little chuckles frequently but without derision. Tunde notices his missing lower teeth and reads that at the time of the interviews he was suffering from severe diabetes and was wheelchair-bound. The wheelchair is not apparent in the videos. Little's language is careful, courtly even (the sparing use of obscenities possibly a reflection of his generation) but in its actual content it is unremittingly obscene. We can't look at evil. We can't look at death, we only think we can. Little objects to being called a rapist though he sexually violated many of the women. For much of his life he has suffered from erectile dysfunction and the sexual excitement comes from strangling his victims usually in the backseat of a car. Trained as a boxer in his youth he beats the women up before killing them. One blow was so severe it broke a woman's spine. Tunde closes his eyes. Why does he persist in watching this?

SITTING IN A TEXAS prison years later Samuel Little is given chalk pastels and he begins to draw the women. He depicts each pair of eyes with or without eyeshadow, each pair of eyebrows, each nose, each mouth, frequently with red lipstick, some of the faces frontal, some in three-quarter view, some in profile, some smiling, all full of attitude. The resulting images are far richer than conventional police sketches, the variety is impressive, the details expert and swift, not at all overworked but with an air of accuracy. Some of the portraits help solve cold murder cases. Each image is somehow, absurdly, "full of life" as though these were faces Little had not only looked at but truly seen, had not only seen but memorized, registered in a moment of lightness and afterwards fully remembered as though the one who did the seeing and the one who did the killing were not one and the same man.

What would someone who was shown these drawings out of context think? They look slightly naive, with elements of folk art and children's art, but there's a precision in them and an intentionality that gives a deeper impression not of naivety but of faux-naivety, of a deft hand and imagination working with ease. They call to mind close-up portraits that are simultaneously skillful and de-skilled by artists like Elizabeth Peyton or Marlene Dumas. Many of the people painted by Dumas are dead and the smudged and vague outlines of her portraits seem to suggest the uncanny distance between the living and the dead. The same is true of the pale portraits painted by Luc Tuymans: some living, some dead, but all seemingly under an unnamed and suffocating existential pressure. The ambiguity between skill and its lack troubles the surface of Tuymans's and Dumas's pictures and Little's as well.

EVERY IMAGE OF A human being proposes a question to the viewer: why am I being shown this? Sometimes, perhaps often, the answer arrives so swiftly that the question is not even noticed: this is a family album, this is a selfie taken on vacation, this is a stock photo for an advertising campaign. But sometimes the question is proposed and the answer is slow in arriving and into this delayed arrival enter unsettling feelings not dissimilar to those one experiences when the camera lingers a little too long on a character's face in a film. The observer thinks and is meant to think: why?

Looking at the drawings Tunde thinks not only of the un-answerable "why" of Little's brutality but also of the elusive "why" of the effect the portraits have on a viewer. As in paintings by Tuymans and Dumas, Little's portraits are even without their backstory haunted by death. Something about them is not up to date. They have life but lack detail, are life-like without being like life. Tunde is reminded that when he sees someone of unremarkable looks in the mainstream media, shown in what is clearly a snapshot or amateur photo-graph with indifferent lighting and in unbeautified color, an image perhaps cropped from a larger image, when he sees such an image printed in *The New York Times* or shown in a television program he immediately thinks: this person is dead. It is a second-order response to the "why" question. In an era of good cameras and publicity stills, when the culture is awash in professional models, professional photographers, makeup artists, and skilled Photoshop retouchers, if the best photo of someone who needs for whatever reason to be pic-tured in the newspapers is a bad photo, there's a good chance that it simply wasn't possible to get a better photo of that person. There's a good chance the person is dead and the reason they are being pictured at all is because they are dead.

Little's portraits are haunted by death. But Tunde does not want to consent to the framing of Little's story under the rubric of "the most prolific serial killer." He is queasy about the heartless triumphalism of that frame which figures the story as entertainment. Little is a real-life avatar of the sexual perversions people love to read about and watch in television series. People—but what about he himself? When he watches police procedurals what is he watching? He is allowing himself to be guided in certain ways that are taken as natural. It is natural to be horrified by a serial killer of women, it is natural to be disgusted by a strangler. But isn't there some consent in being so directed, consent to a certain definition of what constitutes "crime," consent of a coerced sort to the idea that vicious loners are the worst criminals? There are other things that constitute murderous crime, things that do not trigger the same horrified fascination. There are killings carried out under the direction of men who wear suits and live in nice suburbs; killings done by men at computer terminals in nondescript facilities on the outskirts of American towns, and by women too; killings done at vast scale in the name of an economic system. Murder is not limited to merciless human hands on vulnerable human necks. Sometimes it is sufficient to have only the movement of money, the click of a button, the evocation of the legal right to preemptive violence. As for "the most prolific serial killer": what would that even mean in a country built on genocide?

YEARS AGO ANTHONY HAD presented to a group of their friends after a dinner a disturbing set of images. Everybody had eaten well and had had a few drinks and the mood was for strange things from the internet. Anthony showed a Wikipedia page titled "List of unidentified murder victims in the United States." The description was innocuous enough but the page, in addition to accounts of specific crimes and the conditions in which the bodies were found, contained several portraits made by various police departments around the country of these unidentified persons. Because the portraits were reconstructed from grievously damaged faces or decomposed remains and because they had been made with the aid of computer programs they had a hyperreal or surreal appearance. In some cases they looked like Pixar images.

Several of the portraits were made from the remains of people who died decades ago. The Walker County Jane Doe died between October 31 and November 1 in 1980 in Texas. The Odessa Jane Doe was found in Delaware in 1993. The New Castle County John Doe was found in 1994, the Floyd County John Doe in Indiana in 1977. The Popes Island Jane Doe was found in two garbage bags wrapped in a white and teal-colored wool blanket in Massachusetts in 1996. She had been shot twelve times. That night after the dinner party Tunde had nightmares.

He returns to the page now. The images of the unidentified murder victims are more detailed than he remembers. These numerous Jane and John Does are people who are unknown. Their appearance is unconnected to their lives, connected only to their deaths. How does one live a lifetime on this earth to whatever age and on being violently removed from it leave no visible ripple? No one has lived alone. To be human is to be in community. But some die alone and a few die without even their death entering the community of the dead. This is what troubles Tunde about these computer-aided portraits: that with their fake skies and backgrounds, their meticulously rendered hair, their plastic-looking skin, and their intense, almost frantic, gazes, they are images of those who are in some sense undead.

Death in human life only makes sense when death has been acknowledged. It is not a raw biological fact, not for humans. Death is knowledge of death, death is the ritual for the dead. This is why when we hear someone has died we always want to know how it happened: because in order to begin to absorb the pain of the loss we need a narrative. Acknowledging the dead, calling them by their names, and laying them to rest are acts embedded in the deepest layer of human behavior. Among the earliest of all cultural artifacts are burial mounds and barrows.

THE UNCANNY-VALLEY JANE AND John Does lead him to a more recent set of images. In the sibling chat last year Taiwo had sent him and Kehinde a photograph of someone neither of them recognized, a fair-haired white man. This was a game he and the twins sometimes played: challenging one another to figure out what was unusual about a given image. Tunde's guess in this case was that perhaps the "white" man wasn't actually white at all, that he was just a very fair-skinned black person. Kehinde's guess was that the man had not been assigned male at birth. Taiwo wrote back to say that both of those might indeed be the case, there was no way of telling one way or the other. But she had sent this particular photograph because it was of someone who had never existed. The image was entirely computer-generated, she said. She sent them a link to the website. Tunde had glanced at it at the time.

He now returns to the website and spends half an hour on it. "This person does not exist," the URL announces. Each time he refreshes the page a new face appears. A young woman with olive skin and dark brown hair, a middle-aged man with white skin and stubble, a gender-ambiguous person with white skin and gray eyes, a white woman of about fifty with arched eyebrows, an East Asian boy of about ten, an Indonesian-looking girl of about thirteen, a red-haired woman with red lipstick. Ordinary people, some beautiful, some less so, an entire population. The site is run on something called a generative adversarial network. A computer program is given access to a vast archive of human faces, engages in deep learning, and begins to pick up the patterns and varieties of the photographed human face. From what it knows about faces the program is then able to generate new faces ad infinitum.

The program appears to have mastered light and shadow, skin color, hair texture, expression, attitude. The results are impressive and discomfiting. Most of the images do not fall into the uncanny valley as happened with the unidentified murder victims. These people who do not exist in fact look real. Occasionally there are glitches in the rendering and someone's ears are weird or someone has glasses growing out of their temples or the background pattern is incoherent. But generally the photographs are convincing, showing people in a variety of light conditions with a believable range of facial expressions. Some of the pictures are normal and perfectly banal in a way that might in a different context make him think the person was dead. But these ones are not dead, they have simply never lived, they simply never will have been. They are pure algorithmic phantoms, pure phantasms, a third vertex to the two created by Little's sketches of the remembered dead and the police images of the unidentified Jane and John Does: the remembered dead, the remembered undead, the imaginary never-liveds.

MOST OF THE HUMAN BEINGS who have lived and died have left behind them no trace of how they looked, what their voices sounded like, how they moved, what they preferred. It is a vast oblivion but also a relief that we are not inundated with the faces and presences of the innumerable dead. We can move on with our twenty-first-century lives without having to watch videos of every eleventh-century inhabitant of Normandy or Java or Songhay. It was not until the invention and dissemination of photography that it became common for large numbers of people to have their likenesses recorded for posterity, a possibility that had previously been available only to the wealthy and powerful; and it was also only in that era as well with the invention of the gramophone that it became possible for anyone's voice at all, no matter how eminent, to be recorded and heard after their death. The earlier privilege of remaining uncaptured, of dying with one's death, was lost. Should the dead move around us like those who haven't died? Should their presence be more material than those one sees in dreams?

He recalls the advisory note often present in Australian-produced films, addressed to Aboriginal and Torres Strait Islander people, that the film they are about to watch contains the images, voices, and names of deceased persons. This gesture of respect or caution has behind it a cultural practice with which he is not familiar, a taboo against naming the dead. In some Aboriginal and Torres Strait Islander cultures the recently dead are referred to only with circumlocutions. When the technology of photography and film became commonplace in those communities it led to a further discomfort with viewing images of the dead or with hearing their voices. For many Westerners no existential or moral distinction is made between watching a film made ten years ago and one made seventy years ago, even though it is likely that most people in the latter would already be dead. (More than once Sadako has turned to him while they are watching an old film and whispered: all these people are dead.) Looking up the protocols around the Australian advisory notes, Tunde finds a different concept, also used by some Aboriginal people. Because it can be hard to tell if white people are happy or sad, if they are jealous or angry or moody, because the notion of a stiff upper lip is believed to make these public displays of emotion unwelcome for them, some Aboriginal people say "white people have no face." A startling phrase and he can't help but like it. White people have no face. An unwritten poem.

And it is this droll moment that makes him realize what else it is about the computer-generated faces that is bothering him: those faces are almost all white. A very few of them could be read as Asian or Latinx but in thirty minutes of clicking he has landed on not a single black face. White people have no face and that face is everywhere. It is probably a simple instance of algorithmic bias in this case. But he knows these things are never simple. In one sense the people in the photographs can be said to have no race at all, as they are fictional creations, not real people. But that is a language game since these are intended to be taken as people or as photographs of people. The project is implicitly a representation of the world. Why then does this imagined world, a world made by certain technologically minded Americans, have very few black people in it? He is not one to insist on black representation in every context. He is not aware of himself trying to keep score and he finds it fatiguing to even have to notice such things. But that is not entirely true. He does notice, in fact he notices automatically and he finds the absences egregious. It would be more exhausting to shut his eyes to such erasures. He expects that the designers will have excuses about data sets and the availability of material on which to train the generative adversarial network. But there are always excuses and they are often plausible. That granted, what he knows is that white people are comfortable in all-white environments. They don't notice black absence in their museums and schools, in their restaurants, in the movies they watch, the books they read, the scholars they cite. Even in a purely fictional world, even in a futuristic world, their default is monochrome. It is as though to put black people into fiction or to imagine them in the future would be to participate in an unseemly exercise in political balance, as though black presence could only and ever be there to represent "blackness." He can hear himself arguing now and he dislikes the sound of it.

He had thought of Tuymans and Dumas but now he thinks of Lynette Yiadom-Boakye, whose portraits are all of fictional persons. There is an abundance of black presence in Yiadom-Boakye's paintings, black people who do not exist anywhere but in her paintings, paintings that may be set in the past, present, or future. With their loose brushwork and dark palette and a technical approach reminiscent of Goya and Manet her paintings often contain in the same space feelings of ease and melancholy. He feels anchored in the world of these paintings in which invented individuals are full of presence and feeling. Yiadom-Boakye's paintings entail a compassion large enough to summon even those who are not otherwise imagined. They move towards life and more life. They are in this sense opposite to Samuel Little's images of the black women he has methodically murdered. He goes to town, kills a woman, gets out of town. He does this over and over again, often in places he hardly knows. Sometimes he returns to a city and sometimes he attaches himself to one. And in no city does he kill more than he does in Los Angeles. That is where he kills Carol, Guadalupe, Audrey, "Granny," "Alice," "T-Money," and many unnamed others, all of whose faces come to rest in the archive of his mind until he summons them up again in pastels. Perhaps it is this fixation of Little's on Los Angeles that makes Tunde think of his own last visit to L.A. in 2016, a trip he undertook at Yusuf's invitation.

YUSUF WAS TURNING FORTY. He had invited Tunde and ten other friends none of whom lived in Los Angeles (Yusuf didn't either) to spend three days in the city with him. It was a marvelous weekend, the last flower of their youth. Most of the friends were important to Yusuf from various parts of his life but did not really know each other well. Tunde knew Yusuf and two other people there; three or so others he'd heard about. But this newness was what made the gathering so enjoyable. It was a good old-fashioned bender, with the drinking starting early each day at brunch at the house rental in Pasadena and then everyone rambling through streets and museums, shops and outdoor concerts, getting dinner reservations for twelve at some restaurant or the other, and finally ending up at a late-night spot. Tunde had never seen Yusuf so happy and that happiness was contagious. He felt happy too, unaccountably lighter than he'd been in years. About half the crew were married or attached but no one had come with their partners. This gave the gathering some of the sweet innocence of a college trip abroad. Perhaps predictably two of the friends chose to misbehave. One had a wife and three children in Jacksonville, the other was unmarried and loutish. When they began to cling to each other everyone else ignored them, irritated that they had broken such obvious codes. What was anyone to do? The fallout—and there was fallout—came after L.A. and was theirs alone to clean up.

On the final night in the city the crew ended up at the rooftop bar of the Ace Hotel. Around midnight about half the party split off to go elsewhere in the downtown area. Tunde was many drinks into his long weekend. He felt foggy. He saw Máire and Yusuf across the crowded floor. Yusuf was dancing, balancing a glass on his forehead. The music at the bar was skittish, electronic, loud. Tunde had another mezcal cocktail and was losing count. He interrogated himself: how drunk am I, how lucid am I, will I be sober enough to get an Uber, will I be able to find my way back to Pasadena? But soon after his mind was carried by unseen waves and he began to think of you. And it was as though the thought of you suddenly expanded to fill his entire visual field. He tried to think of your face, your voice. He couldn't. You'd been dead three years and he had never lost anyone that close to him before. He tried to think of your face. He couldn't. He tried to remember your voice, you his beloved friend of nearly two decades. He couldn't. The effort to think was a black cloud sitting in his mind, taking up all the space. He called out to you with the voice of his mind and you were not there and his breathing became shallow. He could not remember you. It was as though you had never had a face at all, and tears filled his eyes.

HE SWITCHES OFF THE lamp in the living room and heads upstairs. The storm had been intense but brief. There is an impression of clarity now, of newly washed air. The silent house is his in the dark. He passes the glass door at the landing through which he sees the black sky. Far away, visible as the faintest red blush in the sky, is Mars. Moving across the Gale Crater at this very moment the rover *Curiosity* sends pictures home. It is studying climate and geology on the Martian plane, searching for evidence of water. Many of the pictures *Curiosity* sends arrive in a vignetted format, set within a dark circle as though inside a black cardboard frame. The circular images of ridges and rocks, of petrified weather events and a gentle curved horizon are like multiple views of the vitreous interior of an eye. The photographs are mostly black and white but some of them are rendered in color. Fine dust and a low-pressure atmosphere mean that the daytime sky on Mars would be red to human eyes. Then the Martian day ends and the light of the setting sun travels a greater distance before it is refracted through this alien-to-us atmosphere. The sunsets there are blue.

FOUR

—

SOON AFTER MOVING TO THE HOUSE ON ELLIS STREET THEY decided to use one of the two smaller rooms as their bedroom and the other as a guest room. The large room became her study. It has a high ceiling and a big casement window on the southwest wall overlooking the garden. Because the neighboring house is set well back and because a large shade-casting spruce fell during one of last summer's storms the study is now bright in all seasons including winter. In winter the light is white and cool.

A chestnut-colored desk, an armless leather chair, two white bookcases, a daybed covered with an indigo Sri Lankan cloth. A 1966 photograph of John Coltrane given to her by her dad. A computer, a pair of small speakers, a corkboard. An index card on which she has written in her rapid, angular, right-slanted cursive: *I am deliberate and afraid of nothing—Audre Lorde*. Next to the index card, her business card and on it a phone number in blue ink; whose number, she no longer remembers. A photo of her godson Ting Ting. Two drawings of amaryllis, one drawing of a bunch of ranunculus. The drawings are by her. Above the corkboard a calendar from the New York Botanical Garden. November. It is just past three in the afternoon and she is lying down.

When the opportunity at Vine Pharma came up a few years ago she thought it would be interesting to come back to her home state. She grew up on the North Shore. Her mother and father now live in Acton. Her mother still teaches in the business management program at St. Anthony's as she has for thirty-five years. Her father retired from the same institution in 2015 after a steady journey through the ranks. He was supervisor of evening operations, director of custodial services, and finally vice president of facilities management. Her parents met in Japan in 1970. He was playing cornet with a traveling jazz orchestra and she had just graduated from Waseda. In those unlikely circumstances love happened. Some years later her mother received her PhD from UMass Boston. Her father had always worked with his hands. Through the years people made the assumption that he was ex-military, that she'd met him when he was stationed in Japan. The reality was prosaic in a different way: two gentle souls who recognized each other one night half a century ago and who had never stopped recognizing each other since.

The family consensus is that Masako is more like their dad. Masako is the one who has the career in the music world that eluded him and who shares his lack of interest in university degrees. Hip-hop is her world. From her college days she had a talent for making herself part of that scene, befriending people, getting involved in promotion and management. She has stayed with it though the business has changed and she now works for a large concert promoter. In the mid-nineties all three Fugees spent the night at their home in Gloucester. Her dad had dusted off his cornet and played bebop for them. Sadako, on study abroad in Osaka that year, had missed the moment.

Sadako is more like her mom, according to the same family consensus. Sadako can see how the consensus was reached: the head for math, the talkativeness, the ironic temperament, the doctorate. But she's also the one who physically resembles her dad and, though it could never be admitted, the one he is more fond of. He thinks of her as the "Southern" daughter, in whom he can see Alabama and the tall, loose-limbed, capable women of his family lineage: his cousin Alice, his aunt May, his own mother. Growing up Sadako played his records of music by Minnie Riperton, Chaka Khan, the Commodores, Kimiko Kasai, old-fashioned tastes for which Masako still calls her "grandma."

The natural light in the study is fading. On Sadako's mind is menu planning for Thanksgiving tomorrow. It will be just the four of them, a welcome rarity. Sean is in California with his brother's family and Tunde is en route to Mali. Just the four of them and theirs is not a fractious family. Her parents are affectionate but good with boundaries and she hasn't had a meaningful argument with her sister in more than a decade. They are four different personalities with a common root. Sadako and her mom are quick with the back-and-forth, Masako is more watchful, though not shy, and their dad is laconic. His quietness, Sadako sometimes thinks, is simple amazement: his grandparents were sharecroppers and, look, these are his daughters. Sadako's parents still have their health, mobility, and mental sharpness though she and Masako have noticed that their mom's English which has been excellent their entire lives is falling off a bit, a suggestion their mom dismisses with annoyance. This family of four is the shape Sadako knows best. They will drink sake and play board games. Her parents will stay the night and her sister will drive back to Waltham; but Sadako will try to persuade her to stay as well.

What she has with Tunde is a stable shape too. Mutual attraction, intimacy, loyalty, different tastes certainly, congruent politics. She is analytical and sometimes tempestuous, he is improvisatory and when it suits him inexpressive. He's more obsessed with music but there's their shared reverence for Coltrane. They are practiced at the many microadjustments togetherness requires and by now they mostly know what to do, how to handle each other when analysis becomes rigid or improvisation becomes chaotic. The choice to be child-free has helped, she thinks.

He will have checked in at the airport by now. The ripple back in September seemed to take him by surprise. But that was the problem, that he somehow hadn't seen or sensed what was building up. She loves him for his intelligence and kindness. She loves above all his wish to be good. But a wish is not the same as a will and sometimes she is troubled by how unaware he can be of his failings. She has not put the word "complacency" to it until now. They'd had a frank conversation after she came back from her days at Masako's. They were in agreement that this ripple should not become turbulence. That was where the conversation had begun. They'd had plenty of turbulence before and neither wanted to go through that again.

They talked it over. He wanted clarification on something. Long ago, he reminded her, she had said that no one had given her as much joy in her life as he had and no one had caused her so much pain. He had been taken aback at the time. Now he was asking: was it as bad as that? What could he have done that was so egregious? It hurts as much as it's worth, she said. If something happened to him it would cause her more grief than if it happened to someone else, even more than if it happened to her parents or sister. And for the same reason, because of the depth of her trust in him, the depth of her vulnerability with him, when he hurt her in some way it was more wounding than if someone else did it. Yes, he said, but what have I done to hurt you? She responded: whatever it is, whenever it happens, it counts for more. She wasn't sure she was getting through. She dropped the subject.

But intuiting something pliant underneath his confusion she returned to something else from the past. She reminded him that a couple of years ago she'd said that he did not seem aware of the ways life might be changing for a woman in her forties, the things that might be changing in her body and health, the things she might be sorting through in her mind as she underwent those changes. When she'd said it he'd done the predictable thing which was to defend himself. But when she brought that conversation up again in the aftermath of this ripple she saw that his attitude was now serious. He listened and he asked questions. They were sitting on the sofa during this conversation. He came closer to her and held her as she tried to find her words. At first she was startled, unable to trust his sudden alertness, but soon she eased herself into the knowledge that the things between the words were being heard. No there was no language yet for the little despairs nipping at her heels but now she knew he could receive that inarticulacy. His earnestness, his determination now to be better, felt like warmth. In the weeks that followed, that warmth became a new intimacy, an intimacy expressed in more contact, in exploratory and frequent touching of hands, faces, bodies. It was there in sex but also in their moments of lying naked together. When you find your way back to each other you are mystified that the path was ever lost.

The fallen spruce has created a space in the corner of the garden. She wants to revitalize this open space with sage, rosemary, chives, and thyme. She will line the border with marigolds and black-eyed Susans. Last spring she noticed some sparseness in the flowerbed as well. In October she planted additional tulips and daffodils in those areas. There was rain this past weekend but today is cloudy, warmish. The color from the beds will come up blazing in early May. She taps a red heart emoji into her phone, adds an orange-colored heart to it and a yellow one and a purple one. She considers for a moment then deletes all four. Instead she writes a line from their private lexicon—"you keep me from losing my head"—and sends the message. Then she sends another of the four colored hearts. There's still some paleness in the sky but the room by now is nearly dark. The bulbs are buried in the damp earth.

IN HIS SECOND YEAR of college Tunde lived down the hall from two girls. Teresa was Spanish and Hawa was from Mali and in late October that year both girls had out-of-town visitors. It wasn't clear where Hawa's cousin Madou had traveled from. Teresa's boyfriend Luis, originally from Seville, had come to the U.S. from Cáceres where he was at university. There was a party in the girls' shared suite one Saturday night. Guitars were brought out. Both Madou and Luis could play well and they began to play together. Neither spoke English. They communicated with smiles, nods of the head, and the occasional "aha" and found each other in the language of chords, tunings, and improvisations. Luis's playing had flamenco inflections in it. Madou's had bits of rumba and highlife. Borrowing riffs, taking up suggestions from each other's lines, together they made a third thing, a thing that had never been heard before. Laughter, delight, conjuration, a marvel spun out of insubstantial air. Tunde was moved by it. Listening to them he found himself imagining a map and the music, changing as it traveled from Mali to Mauritania to Algeria, Morocco, and Spain. He thought of vast stretches of desert across which the secrets of music were ferried as carefully as water or gold, the musicians like men who knew the secret of finding moisture or digging wells. This unlikely meeting in a Michigan dorm room was retracing some extraordinary span of human experience. The music entered his soul, made him resonate and when it ended after half an hour he felt he was returning to earth.

Twenty-six years have passed. He has forgotten so much: faces, last names. He might as well have dreamed it. But he has never forgotten that night's glimpse of musical heaven. A few months after Madou and Luis's visit, in the spring of 1994, he accompanied Selçuk to a record shop in downtown Bronson. Selçuk had a rich knowledge of music and an untiring desire to evangelize that love. That day he wanted to buy *A Meeting by the River,* Ry Cooder's project with V. M. Bhatt. The acoustics on that album were out of this world, Selçuk said. Cooder with his guitar and Bhatt with his modified veena had met at a chapel in rural Texas late one night for the recording which was made with few microphones and registered direct to tape. Tunde was taken with Selçuk's enthusiasm and was later to spend many hours listening to the album. But that afternoon at the record shop he happened to see another album in which Cooder was involved, a new release called *Talking Timbuktu,* the lead guitarist on which was Ali Farka Touré, whom at the time Tunde had not heard of. The memory of Madou and Luis's playing possibly guided his will. He examined the CD. He could barely afford the eighteen-dollar price but he felt with what seemed to him a mystical intuition that he could afford even less not to take the CD home.

THERE ARE TIMES LISTENING to music on the radio or by streaming when he is tempted to identify what he is hearing by looking up the track name. He resists the impulse and does something else: he turns up the volume or lowers it. The main thing in such moments is to reorient his attention and remove any extramusical information, anything that might get in the way of his direct contact with the music, and focus instead on the immediate experience. Everyone arrives at knowledge of the world from a personal point of view and is not the poorer for it. Each person understands life on the basis of small personal events. Firsthand experience is what matters. It is by being grounded in what we know and what we have experienced that we can move out into greater complexities. When possible he wants to listen and receive the music in his body before he gives it a name.

Singing began in ritual with the purpose of demarcating sacred time from ordinary time. It fortified the web of human relationships, strengthening the connections between a human community and the universe in which that community found itself. Then there was an expansion from what people could do with their voices into the larger sense of music that included instruments. To say that ancient people took pleasure in their music is not to say that they made music for the sake of pleasure. Music had holy purpose much the same as cave paintings or carved figurines and evolved like those visual arts with the needs of human societies. And then in time, in the syncopated time that brings revolution to places when they are ready for it, music came to speak of the deeds of deified ancestors and divine kings and it became one of the means by which narrative privileges won in battle were transferred from one generation to the next. Intimacy and grandeur: both are woven into the prehistory of music, both have survived through its history. All this affects our listening now at the far end of that history. The captain announces that departure will be soon. A text arrives from Sadako, and a second. He responds in their accustomed way—"without you, I would lose my footing"—following it up with a kissing emoji. Then he adjusts the fit of his headphones and increases the volume.

OFTEN WHEN HE IS entertained by music he is also displeased by having been entertained, as though he had forgotten something or gotten something wrong, as though he has let someone down. In those moments when the listening is shallow he perceives a distance between what he hears and what it means. He is aware of an attitude of the spirit to which he sometimes has access and sometimes doesn't. What was inaugurated by the long-ago encounter with Madou and then by the purchase of *Talking Timbuktu* was a love that led him to countless hours of listening to recordings and took him to many concerts in many countries over the years. He gained a certain listening expertise in what people in the U.S. and Europe call "world music." Recent years have subtly inflected that love. No longer is the music of Mali (and Guinea, the Gambia, and the entire sphere of Manding cultural influence) something he simply enjoys with whatever depth of intensity. It is now an acoustic amulet averting evil from him. The music shields him. Could that be true, that it shields him? Isn't there something weak in this as a response to bright unbearable reality? But he knows it shields him, he knows he is defended by it as a private protection that he can hardly speak about without seeming to be speaking about something else. The defense it affords him is a lonely one conveyed in languages he does not know but that he emotionally comprehends. These languages tell him that the material reality in which he exists is not where his spirit is best nurtured. His material world is set in the center of white learning. He is in the center of that and he flowers in it, not without some doubt, not without some shame. But he knows that he can only do so because there is another life into which his roots are sunk, a life to which he has access through language, through dance, through music. He has tried to speak of this and has failed perhaps in the way Mau Piailug might fail in describing his experience of the sea or the way he himself might fail at describing why Mau is significant to him. He has noticed that when he attempts to put the experience of this music into words his words are received as categories: the category of music as entertainment, the category of anthropological interest, the category of good taste, the category of unusual taste, the category of racial solidarity, the category of being a stranger in someone else's home. He wants to say no to all this, that he means to convey experience not categories but he can never seem to find the words of the right accuracy or sufficient intensity. But why should he wish to translate to others the thought that something untranslatable is happening to him? Let the untranslatable remain untranslatable. Let the thing that makes him feel less alone remain one of the things in which he feels most alone.

The sound of the kamale ngoni, the njarka, the kora, the guitar, the balafon, certain voices imbued with gestures going back, it is said, to the time of Sundiata Keita. Every time he hears these sounds he is back in Mali though he has never been to Mali. He is restored to his place in the web of time and put in contact with his ancestors. How can this be so, since his literal ancestors are not from Mali? His own people are Yoruba and he calls on that tradition for ancestral help as well. But lineage is a forest of forking paths.

The truth of his parents and their parents and their parents is an ancestral truth. He is of the line of Esude. Another ancestral truth is the way the cells in his body respond when certain music enters him. Everything he would like to say about his experience of the world is encapsulated in certain songs, not popular at the center where he lives, not known to most of the people around him. When he dies will the person in charge of the arrangements know what music to play? Even Sadako, were she to survive him, would have only a general idea of the intensity of his identification with certain sounds, and surely the reverse must be true: he knows only in broad outline what sustains her most deeply and intimately. In the six-minutes-and-six-seconds duration of "Fanta Barana," the soaring and imperfect tenor of Lafia Diabaté accompanied by the rolling melodies of the acoustic guitars of Djelimady Tounkara and Bouba Sacko, in that mid-tempo song recorded in a warm and natural ambience in Bamako one night in 1993, he feels as though the lightning of that other night in 1993 at Bronson College with Madou and Luis had been captured in a bottle. The music interprets him. That shadowy voice and those unamplified guitars set a contour around his body and he becomes legible again to himself. What he loses sight of for long periods in the glare of his life becomes visible again. Never mind what will be played at his funeral, what counts is what he's heard in his life, what he's hearing now as the plane's engines finally begin to rumble and the cabin darkens.

IT IS HOT OUTSIDE but the interior of the hotel is cooled by unseen air-conditioning units. The lobby is large and hums with quiet talk. Every other person wears dark shades. The floors are off-white marble and beyond the entryway there is a seating area with furniture upholstered in black and white bogolan fabric. Businessmen in suits and traditional gowns come and go. A woman in a magnificent pink boubou flows past the front desk and towards the elevators. A man in a black suit hurries after her wheeling three pieces of luggage. Hotels are places of power and a hotel like the Grand Bamako is especially a place of power because of its stark contrast with the world outside. Outside are the women selling food, the men in the taxicabs awaiting fares. But even in the lobby he feels his particular apartness: his American passport, the fact that he is checking in in English, his lightweight and light-colored jacket, his violet scarf.

He likes to arrive at a place and be conveyed from the airport to the hotel and receive a keycard and ascend the elevators and enter a room that looks almost exactly the same wherever he might be in the world. The man at the desk at the Grand Bamako tells him his room is not yet ready. Tunde asks where he can get some lunch and the man directs him to the hotel restaurant behind the seating area on the other side of the lobby. He leaves his suitcase at the front desk and as he crosses the lobby he sees three tall white men in military fatigues standing by the bank of elevators.

In the evening he wakes up from a nap. His dear old friend Naïny comes to meet him at the Grand clapping with excitement as he walks across the lobby. She used to live in New York when he lived there too and then she moved to Madrid. Together they walk outside the hotel's compound to the taxi stand. The man they hire, young and eager, is named Adama. Naïny whose French is fluent does the negotiating. Crossing the River Niger in Adama's decrepit car Tunde's heart swells. He has never seen the Niger before not even from a plane and this is the river that gave Nigeria its name, the originary river of West African history. The bridge is busy in early dusk, hectic with taxis and motorbikes. When Adama drops them off at the arts canteen Naïny takes his phone number.

Several of the artists and curators who have come to town for the photography Biennial are at the canteen. They've come from the U.S., from Spain, France, Germany, Nigeria,

Ghana. Tunde knows many of them. Laurie has flown in from Paris and she rushes around the table to wrap him in an embrace. Food arrives from the kitchen, there's laughter and the evening feels like a beautiful memory even as it unfolds. Sitting at the long table at the canteen Tunde has a vision of himself at a table in Bamako. The lighting is low. A peeling mural on the walls depicts epic scenes featuring a river, a village, a siege, a series of turrets. It is late when Naïny calls Adama to come pick them up. He drops Naïny off at her hotel and then he brings Tunde back to the Grand. As they approach the hotel Tunde manages conversation with his broken French. At the mention of music Adama says that his family name is Tounkara and that the great guitarist is his uncle. A distant uncle but Tunde is still startled. Adama says that clans are large in Mali and that many families are connected. When Tunde returns to his room he feels a compulsion to listen to Djelimady Tounkara again. He selects "Bastan Toure" from the *Bajourou* album. That song reminds him of another so he goes onto YouTube and begins to listen to a variety of renditions of "Nanfoulé," one of the standards of the Mandinka repertory. His jet lag has now swerved over into a stubborn wakefulness. There's the painfully beautiful version by Diaou Kouyaté supported by guitars and koras. There's Mah Kouyaté's rocking mid-tempo interpretation, there's Mori Djely Kouyaté with a French pianist, there are versions by Manda Sira, Kani Dambakaté, Fatoumata Kamissoko. Deeper and deeper he goes. There's the great Kanté Manfila in a poorly recorded television clip. There's Mory Kanté's high-energy pop version. These names, these voices fill his heart: to be here in Mali and be in real time with something towards which he has been drawn for so long is a joy so intense that his heart feels melancholy at it. He listens to the deeply concentrated version of the song the revered Guinean singer Mahawa Kouyaté recorded in the early 1980s and it is in the mists of her incantation that sleep comes to him.

THE TRIP WAS NOT long in the planning. He is supposed to be in Santiago at this moment but an uprising broke out there and Chileans turned out in the streets in their hundreds of thousands to demand a better life. The uprising meant that his planned lecture was postponed. And so at short notice he decided to travel instead to Bamako. The Biennial is his pretext but long-nursed desire is his reason. He has just under a week to devote to the journey, the time between his Tuesday classes before and after Thanksgiving.

The flight is via Paris as is the case with most international flights to Bamako. But now in Bamako he remembers his last time in Paris. It was summer. He was with Laurie and they had gone to the Louvre. They'd come out at the glass pyramids in the late afternoon. Earlier that day walking around Place de la Concorde while Laurie was at work Tunde had seen some men selling trinkets. Among the most common items for sale were small die-cast Eiffel Towers. The rows of little towers on white sheets and the fact that all the sellers were black men reminded him of an excellent photograph that had been made in precisely such a context by Alessandra Sanguinetti. Sanguinetti's photograph had shown a single arm reaching out from the right side of the image to place a small Eiffel Tower onto the white cloth spread on the sandy gravel. Two corners of the cloth were held down by towers and in the middle of the cloth, in the middle of the picture, was a jumble of the towers in a variety of sizes and finishes: pewter, brass, black, gold. It was a simple but memorable photograph, compact as a koan. Confronted with a scenario just like it Tunde wanted to make a photograph that rhymed with Sanguinetti's but he didn't have a proper camera with him, only his phone. He tried anyway, drawn by the play of scale and visual rhythm. The sellers didn't pay him any attention as he took a few shots. Finding none of the resulting pictures interesting he went on his way.

Later when he and Laurie came out of the Louvre he saw another group of vendors. This time they did not have cloths set down. The Eiffel Towers hung in clusters from their arms. Tunde took out his phone almost by instinct to worry the photographic problem further. He took two photographs of the towers carried by one vendor. Even as he took the photos he knew he would be stymied by the limitations of the phone. In any case he hadn't done enough work to resolve the visual problem and allow his images to stand on their own. Seldom did he take a photo in a hurry and later on find it worth keeping. Due time and consideration were almost always necessary. This record of failure did not stop him from taking hurried photos from time to time.

As Laurie turned to ask if he had any ideas about where to go for dinner someone grabbed him by the arm. For a second he thought they were being robbed. Then he saw that it was the man whose goods he had just photographed. Tunde shook him off. The man was slim, tall, and very dark and his eyes bulged in anger. He demanded that Tunde delete the photos. Taken aback Tunde was silent at first then he refused the demand. He told the man he had photographed objects not his face. The man grabbed Tunde's upper arm again and his mates came around urging him on, stoking the sudden fire. Tunde insisted he had not photographed the man. They demanded his phone. Laurie spoke rapidly in French to the men. Tunde shook himself free. The man continued to shout and flecks of his spittle fell on them as they walked away.

He sees these men as his brothers. Each time he sees informal black traders in Europe he considers himself on their side against all the hostility they experience. At least that's the story he has convinced himself of. But to this brother at the Louvre he was no brother. That he was Nigerian, that Laurie was African American, that the man himself was probably Senegalese, what difference did that make? The man saw nothing but a class enemy. Selling trinkets at the Louvre was a precarious life and possibly he had no papers, possibly he was part of a network in which he was indentured. Whatever profits he made from long days out in the sun were surely meager. Why should someone take a photograph of him, of his goods? He was furious not only because a photo might endanger him but because he had been given nothing in exchange. Tunde hadn't bought anything, hadn't asked for permission, hadn't paid for the right, hadn't even considered doing so. Here was a stranger who had simply looked past him and taken something the way the wealthy take what belongs to others and then act surprised when they are challenged. Taking. That's what those who are well-off do. They take and take and take.

HOW IS ONE TO live without owning others? Who is this world for? White people taught us that the world could be dominated by means of religion and warfare, collected for the sake of pleasure and scholarship, possessed through travel, and owned by anyone willing to claim and defend that ownership. How is one to live in a way that does not cannibalize the lives of others, that does not reduce them to mascots, objects of fascination, mere terms in the logic of a dominant culture? The more expansive his interests in the world the more urgent these questions become. "Travel photography," "travel writing": they have become dead terms and he can't make them live. Walking through the Medina Koura in the center of Bamako with the camera in his hand he wonders what photographs of such a place can even be. He often tells his students that there is no such thing as a good photograph, not if such a judgment is based merely on how pretty an image is. It matters, he tells them, who made the photograph and what afterlife it has beyond the moment in which it was made. Sometimes the students object. Is he saying that a white person can never photograph in Africa? Isn't it the right of the artist to make art, to obey the inner creative urges from which any worthwhile art emerges? He turns the question around to them: who taught you that your rights are more important than other people's rights? The excuses made for the display of African bodies are familiar to him. Those excuses are sometimes blunt and unconvincing and sometimes seductive. One well-known white photographer makes mockingly exploitative work but in presenting it always appends a statement that the work is intended to "overturn stereotypes." Everywhere in contemporary photography is the same old vampirism but now it is smart enough to come with good wall text.

———

IN BAMAKO HE GETS an email from your son Lucas. They have met only once before, years ago, but now Lucas writes out of the blue. He and his family have just moved to Boston. He wonders if Tunde has advice about living in New England and suggests meeting up for lunch. But the meeting will not really be about advice, thinks Tunde to himself. It will be, they both must tacitly know, to satisfy a curiosity. One seeking to know this person who was so close to his father, the other wanting to know something about the son of his dear friend. Tunde writes back and says it might be possible to meet up in early December or, if not, in January. Lucas responds warmly and they put the correspondence on pause.

THE CITY IS HOT. The shops have on them names like Coulibaly, Kanté, Touré, Traoré, Keita, names familiar to him, names he has known through the years as the names of musicians, football players, scholars, artists, names redolent of another world with which he feels intimate but from which he has always been distant; and here they are in their ordinary contexts on shop signs and billboards, the material reality of the dream he's been having for almost three decades. He goes to see the exhibitions in the Biennial. Outside one of the venues he sees more white men in military fatigues. These ones, he is able to determine, are Serbian, part of the French-led anti-jihadist force soon to be shipped north. In that far corner of Mali they will drop bombs that will never be accounted for. They will kill people for whom no obituaries will be written.

The market is noisy and things are arranged in the stalls in a manner that shows evidence of various ways of making do and getting by. Fair to call it precarity, fair to think of it a different way and call it agility. When he sees oranges displayed on a plastic sacking on the ground he finally makes a photograph. And then he makes another, of crocodile ornaments on a monumental gate near the old railway station. Through these days he and Sadako are writing to each other, back in their element and ease. He sends her a portrait made of him by an itinerant photographer. She writes back to say that he looks really happy in the portrait and that this makes her happy. She sends back a picture of herself on a ski trip in Vermont with friends.

AFTER DINNER HE TRIES to find out where he can hear some live music. It's not easy. This isn't Lagos or Dakar. After dusk on a Friday Bamako is somnolent. The city is resistant to tourism in a way that he appreciates. He enlists Laurie and Naïny for help and asking around they are told of a place called the Chameleon Club in a residential neighborhood just off the Avenue de l'Indépendance. Laurie has to shake off a German curator whose company they don't want. Then they call Adama whose face betrays his delight at these days of steady work and he takes them there.

Before the journey Tunde had read what he could of contemporary Mali. In every piece the recurring word was "poor" and each time he encountered the word he felt both himself and the country flattened by the term. Poor in what? There was no connection made in any of what he read between Mali's poverty and France's wealth. And yet at the Medina Koura he had seen a demonstration calling on the French to leave, calling on the Malian elite to serve their people instead of foreign governments. If anger at the asymmetrical relationship between Mali and France is missing from the Western press it isn't missing from the streets of Bamako. Here the colonial wound is livid compared to Nigeria where it is a less immediate concern, where there aren't protest marches asking the British to stop interfering.

When they arrive at the Chameleon Club the street is silent. Two men sit as though half asleep under a tree in front of the single-story building. But as they approach the building Tunde hears the feedback of an amplified band. They enter an interior space with an open courtyard around which is a covered terrace. There are few guests, not more than a dozen, seated under the terrace, the tables in front of them clustered with empty beer bottles. The band onstage led by an electric guitar is playing music that he recognizes right away, a cover of Bako Dagnon's "Titati." The vocalist is a young woman in majestic purple "Guinea" cloth ("Guinea" is what this shiny dyed cotton is called in Yoruba; he doesn't know the Bambara name for it). A mural running along the dimly lit walls of the venue features the greats of contemporary Malian music. The mural has paintings of Toumani Diabaté, Kassé Mady Diabaté, Ali Farka Touré, Salif Keita, Bako Dagnon, a kind of hall of fame. The names on the shop signs and now these faces: the familiarity is for him a homecoming and an unsettling. The music pouring from the stage is too loud he thinks at first but soon he experiences it as an immersive wash. This is not an acoustic set at a café, it is not nice background music, it is not the pair of kora players he saw the previous night at a Biennial event whose delicate rendition of "Salimou" was drowned out by the chatter of attendees. Here at the Chameleon he comes to the thought that a certain idea of life requires a certain volume. The singer's voice carries hundreds of years of tradition, the lead guitarist is fleet-fingered, his notes drenched in feedback, the bassist is locked into a groove that rolls forward without wasted effort, and the blind keyboardist pounces on his keys percussively as though he were playing a balafon.

An hour later the young woman begins to sing "Nan-foulé." Life sometimes is in a mood for coincidences and won't let it go. Naïny goes into the middle of the courtyard and begins dancing. The song is said to have been first performed in the 1940s under colonial rule by a djeli who had been arrested and tortured by the French. "Set me free," he sang, "take off these shackles." This singer's rendition is full of yearning and focus. She lowers her voice then spins out a soaring phrase before dropping again with perfect control into a lower register. Naïny floats on that voice like a boat on a sea, a voice bigger than she is, a voice to which she has surrendered. The cumulative effect of the performance is at once uplifting and devastating. Afterwards Tunde goes to the singer and tells her how much he enjoyed her voice and his gratitude for the surprise of hearing a song he had been thinking about. He asks her for her name. When the singer, who now looks much younger than she did onstage, says "Bako Dagnon," he thinks his uncertain French has been misunderstood. He clarifies the question. The singer, smiling, repeats the name and says the late famous Bako Dagnon was her mother. Astonished all Tunde can do is open up his wallet and give young Bako twenty thousand CFA francs in homage.

Other people's lives. They are not subsidiaries, they are not symbols, they are not to be collected. Do the white soldiers at the hotels know this? Could it have occurred to them to believe any of the life they see around them, do they even see any of it? But to talk about them and their greed, their sorcery, seems to him a bad use of his time here. Think instead, he says to himself, of all the people in the Medina Koura, think of them in their homes, in their beds, think of their quotidian worries about their children's schooling. Think about their secret savings, and their delightful subterfuges, their religion and transgressions, their necessary severity, the warmth of their families, and the untranslatable consolations of their lives.

THE LIFE OF SUNDIATA KEITA, legendary founder of the Mali empire, has the shape and rhythm of myth: the unpromising hero who stays in his mother's womb for twelve years; the hero who is prophesied to take the throne, whom the old king attempts and fails to kill in infancy; the hero who refuses to walk until he is aged fourteen and who one day pulls himself upright by grabbing onto a baobab tree, uprooting it in the process. Sundiata is a Muslim but he is immersed in the world of magic and the power of his story is due to the tectonic encounter between these realities. The narrative thrust of the *Epic of Sundiata*, deployed in different ways by different djeli, is always towards Sundiata's confrontation with his enemy Sumanguru,

Lord of the Susus. And this battle is one that is conducted and won not by mere force of arms but by magical prowess.

Almost all versions of the Sundiata legend credit his sister with using a bed trick to help him defeat Sumanguru. Sources agree that she was famous for her beauty but they do not agree on her name. Banna Kanute calls her Nene Faamaga. Bamba Suso calls her Nyakhaleng Juma Suukho. Whatever she is called, she offers herself in marriage to Sumanguru but in the bedroom on the night of the wedding she won't let him touch her. Instead she peppers him with questions about the secret of his strength. The questions are a test of his love for her, a test of his desire.

HE RETURNS TO THE Chameleon Club the next night accompanied by his friends and by Laurie's annoying German, Paul, who turns out to be less annoying than previously thought. They return the night after that with an even larger group. He wanders the city by day, looks at photographs at the Biennial, attends screenings and talks, makes his own photographs, but he comes to understand that his real reason for being in Bamako is these nights in the Chameleon Club. Whatever the size of the audience he feels the bands are playing for him alone. Clans are manifest to a degree he didn't anticipate: he sees performances by Oumou Sangaré's cousin, Toumani Diabaté's brother, Kassé Mady Diabaté's brother. He experiences these families in their extended networks, witnesses the way mastery is a matter of honor for these people who do music as well as anyone anywhere on earth does anything. No they are not doing it for him, they are doing it for themselves and he has been made welcome to listen.

On that third night the crowd is large, the music is for dancing, and he is swept up in it, can hardly find language to describe it. And while he is dancing the thought quickly comes and quickly goes about how he would tell you about the experience. He thinks about how he would describe to you the exquisite embodiment at the heart of it. You were not a dancer but you were a listener and he wishes he could tell it to you. The thought passes over him as lightly as the shadow of a falling leaf.

THE NIGHTS AT THE Chameleon later remind him of something else. Perhaps more modest but "modest" is the wrong word for something that is in its own way so special. In August 2001 he had just returned from London and you had come to New York City from Chicago for two weeks of research. He told you that his relationship with Sandro had ended recently. You had seen that Ali Farka Touré was coming to the city for one of the last stops on his farewell tour. You bought the tickets without even asking Tunde, at prices you knew he wouldn't have been able to afford, an expense worth it because neither of you had seen Ali Farka Touré live before. You loved the music but you knew he loved it even more; it was he who had introduced you to it. Music was the emotional core of the friendship. Through the years whenever you happened to be in the same city together you tried to see concerts and had seen some extraordinary ones: Ahmad Jamal in Chicago, Lizz Wright there too. Once, in London, Alfred Brendel. Music was one of the places where you met. You can't be in Bamako now, you can't be anywhere, but you were in New York back then, back when you were still inside the fabric of time. That night Touré's longtime associate Afel Bocoum played a rootsy opening set and then the maestro himself came onstage cracking jokes to begin with before plunging into the depths. His heavily electrified guitar almost sounding like surf rock summoned up the spirits and filled up the auditorium. And when he laid aside the guitar and played his njarka, the instrument he first taught himself before the guitar, the sense of divination became even more intense. You held your breaths together and followed the wail of that single-stringed fiddle. Hundreds of strangers were having a collective experience. The border between this world and the next became translucent.

A few years later when he heard that Ali Farka Touré had died he wrote to you. He told you of how by coincidence he had been listening to *Niafunké* the entirety of the previous day. These coincidences were always happening to him. You wrote back. Then he phoned and you talked for a long time about that night of the concert in New York City years earlier. He said Touré's funeral cortege in Niafunké had been caught up in a massive dust storm. You said the djinns were grieving one of their own or welcoming him home. Such are the things we say about death to the ones who are nearest to us. We speak this way because the present is infinite, always infinite, from the point of view of all we cannot yet know.

SUNDIATA'S SISTER TELLS SUMANGURU she is puzzled. Why does every army that comes against him fail? Sumanguru says his father was a djinn. Two women conceived him, he says. When he was growing inside the one she was healthy and the other was sick. When he was inside the other she was healthy and the first was sick. The mothers alternated like that until one of them gave birth to him. He divulges this but now his birth mother overhearing her son from outside the bedroom warns him not to give all his secrets away to a "one-night woman." But bedrooms make people wayward. Sumanguru gives the old woman palm wine to make her sleep and this puts a stop to her interference.

Sumanguru tells Sundiata's sister everything or almost everything. How to kill his father the djinn and what would happen if Sumanguru's kingdom were invaded. If the kingdom were invaded he would become a whirlwind. If the army entered that whirlwind with swords he would become an African fan palm. If they tried to fell the palm he would become an ant hill. If they tried to destroy the ant hill he would become a Senegal cou— He pauses mid-phrase and reaches for Sundiata's sister. Before he can touch her she slips his grasp and escapes the palace. And this is how the final battle goes, Sundiata attacking with magic and Sumanguru changing form from whirlwind to fan palm to ant hill until he becomes a Senegal coucal and flies away. This is how Sumanguru escapes because he does not finish revealing his final form as the Senegal coucal to Sundiata's sister and this is how Sundiata Keita takes over the territory of the Susus and comes to the throne of the Manding kingdom.

THE DAY BEFORE HE is to leave Tunde goes to the Grand Marché with Laurie. He buys a pair of brass ci wara. They are not as elegant as the wooden one he bought in Maine. At about a foot high each they are also nowhere near its size. But because he is buying them in Bamako they feel talismanic.

There is no doubt they've been made for the tourist trade and this is what he most likes about them because now the exchange seems transparent and fair. He buys a handmade leather bag for Sadako. Laurie knows the Grand Marché well and takes him to a favorite cloth merchant. In the shop is a large decorative loom-woven piece that could be used as a hanging or as a bedspread. It has a pattern of red, yellow, and green strips with a black and white grid in the middle. The man at the shop is old. He has a white goatee and wears a full-length blue gown and there is a quiet worldliness about him. He tells Laurie and Tunde of his travels in San Francisco, St. Louis, Paris. His untroubled spirit is very different from that of the eager young men at the market who are aggressive with potential customers. Laurie helps Tunde bargain for the cloth. The woven cloth is so substantial and so beautiful. The old man drops the price a bit but won't go below one hundred thousand CFA francs. He is certain of the quality of his cloth and Tunde, willingly charmed by the old man's confidence, buys it.

ON HIS LAST NIGHT he carefully folds the large bright cloth and places the two metal ci wara into its folds. Tomorrow Adama Tounkara will take him to the airport. It doesn't matter where one lives, how cold or hot it is there, how poor it is thought to be, how far away (far away from where?), all that matters is one's people. All that matters is one's accompaniment. But that is not a resolved thought either. Does being with one's people mean the possibility of traveling to see them? Does it mean having them living across town or next door? Does it mean phone calls, text messages, videoconferencing? His people. Not only those he loves but those with whom he would wish to build a life. Those in whose presence he feels yes, this is life. But wait, that is not all that matters. To be contained within oneself matters too and it matters as much. To be integral and to be peopled in balance.

He feels healed by this journey and he doesn't want to leave yet. He wishes he could travel northeast from Bamako through the Sahel to Timbuktu. It is a journey he would have made if the country were not in such a dangerous mood. The journey would take him through the traditional lands of Dogon people in the Bandiagara Escarpment. From their houses on the escarpment Dogon people studied the skies for centuries, carefully tracking the movements of the moon, Saturn, Jupiter, and the brightest star in our sky, Sirius A. An unsolved mystery is how these ancient astronomers were able without telescopes or modern equipment to detect and theorize the existence of Sirius A's companion star Sirius B. Orders of magnitude dimmer than Sirius A, Sirius B is invisible to the naked eye. One theory is that Dogon astronomers reasoned that a star like Sirius A could not go unaccompanied and so, sight unseen, they deduced the orbit of Sirius B. The second star is there because in accordance with their cosmological principles it has to be. Doubleness is the first condition. Says Chinua Achebe, "Wherever something stands, something else will stand by it." Sings Ali Farka Touré, "Honey does not only taste good in one mouth."

FIVE

Aᴿᴇ ᴡᴇ ʀᴇᴄᴏʀᴅɪɴɢ ɴᴏᴡ? ʏᴇs? ᴏᴋ. ᴏɴᴄᴇ ᴀɢᴀɪɴ ɢᴏᴏᴅ ᴇᴠᴇ-
ning everyone and again my heartfelt thanks to my friend
Rae Fazlizadeh for the protective kindness of their wonderful
introduction. I have no hope of living up to it but that is the
way it is with introductions. Thank you Rae.

I begin with one of the better-known paintings in the collection. It surprises me each time I'm here. I remember many
other things but my mind blanks this one out until I enter a
large room in which there are a great many paintings. Depending on which of the entrances I'm using I either see it in
the distance or suddenly to my left and only on seeing it do I
remember: this is here. The painting grabs hold of me in an
unpleasant way. I'm talking about J. M. W. Turner's *Slave
Ship (Slavers Throwing Overboard the Dead and Dying, Typhoon Coming On)*. No encounter with this painting can be
pleasant. Its details are terrible and its full title directs our
looking, telling us to focus first on the grisly foreground and
then on the roiling weather in the background. The title volunteers a great deal of information as though it were speaking itself out of a state of alarm or frenzy. In fact both the
painting and its title are excessive, they overspill. And perhaps it is this feeling of excess, this feeling of obscene over-
muchness, that makes one repeatedly forget that it is indeed
right here just around the corner, just in the distance. We
forget the *Slave Ship*, we must forget the *Slave Ship* in the

way we must forget many difficult things with the kind of forgetfulness that allows us to keep on living our lives.

I now interrupt myself with a small but crucial consideration, because now that I've said it several times, I realize that I am troubled by the title *Slave Ship*. It's the word "slave": a word which still strikes the ear like a lash. There are those who enslave others and there are those who are enslaved by others. But there's no one whose essence or true description is "slave." A person can be enslaved, can be trapped in the death-in-life known as slavery, but that is not who they are. It is something intolerable that is happening to them or that happened to them. For this reason I think that part of the original title is more accurate: *Slavers Throwing Overboard the Dead and Dying*.

The painting was completed in 1840. It is an imaginative reconception of a real event from almost sixty years earlier which Turner had read about in Thomas Clarkson's *The History and Abolition of the Slave Trade*. In 1781 the captain of the slaving ship *Zong*, an inexperienced former ship surgeon named Luke Collingwood, had lost his way on the journey from the West African coast to Jamaica. What was meant to be a six-week journey took him eighteen weeks. After dozens of the hundreds of enslaved people on board had died of sickness and thirst, after dozens of others had committed suicide, Collingwood intentionally threw overboard a hundred and fifty of the living. His notion was to eventually collect the insurance money for human cargo lost at sea rather than risk arriving at port with what to him would have been damaged goods. "Human cargo," "damaged goods": these words are difficult to say.

In Turner's painting the sky is a riot of reds and yellows, stippled with orange, pink, purple, blue, and white. The painting depicts a sunset in a tempest though it's unlikely that the mass murder on the real *Zong* took place during a tempest. The sky in Turner's painting looks as though it is on fire. His seascapes often depict a natural world in a state of wildness beyond human control. The oncoming typhoon as imagined by Turner in this painting will compound the miseries of those in the water. The lurid colors of this sky are not denotative, they are simply atmospheric effects of the kind Turner frequently employed and part of what drew the critic John Ruskin to his work.

In the first volume of his *Modern Painters* Ruskin praised *Slavers Throwing Overboard the Dead and Dying*, which he once owned, as the single work he would choose on which to rest Turner's immortality. Ruskin's praise was essential to the subsequent fame of the work and it also contained that flashiest of allusions to Shakespeare: "incarnadines the multitudinous sea." Mark Twain, meanwhile, described the painting as a lie for the way it showed things like floating iron chains and other impossibilities. "Cat having a fit in a platter of tomatoes," he wrote. Twain was being iconoclastic, his favored mode, but he was not entirely wrong. There is something ungainly, ugly even, about *Slavers Throwing Overboard the Dead and Dying*, an ugliness due not only to the horror of the subject matter. There are other paintings by Turner which are no less bold but which are visually more resolved. One such is his early masterpiece *Dido Building Carthage, or the Rise of the Carthaginian Empire*, painted in 1815. Another is *The Fighting Temeraire, Tugged to Her Last Berth to Be Bro-*

ken Up, painted in 1838. The "importance" of *Slavers Throwing Overboard the Dead and Dying* has over the years cast a
veil over its technical limitations. The hands rising out of the
water are dreamlike, unbearably sad, but look at the sinking
leg on the bottom right: it is too large, it is out of proportion.
Meanwhile the ravenous fish are cartoonishly depicted alongside seagulls and frothing blood, a cartoonishness that dulls
the edge of imagination. These visual solecisms are perhaps
what confused William Makepeace Thackeray and led him to
say, "Is the painting sublime or ridiculous? Indeed, I don't
know which."

But it is easy to get mired in arguments about the technical achievement of a painting. Behind this painting, after all,
is real horror. And that incident itself, the wastage of human
life in the pursuit of an insurance payout, almost seems to
render language useless. It is this impossibility, this failure of
language, that M. NourbeSe Philip takes as the subject of her
extraordinary book-length poem *Zong!* That's *Zong,* the
name of the ship, followed by an exclamation point. In the
remarkable essay she has written as an afterword to the poem
Philip returns time and again to the idea that this is "the story
that cannot be told." The story cannot be told, she says, but
it must be told and it can only be told by not being told. And
so she tells the story that cannot be told in a "language of
grunt and groan, of moan and stutter." Open *Zong!* to almost
any page and you are confronted with a spray of fragmented
phrases, free floating words, isolated morphemes. The face
of the text looks like a net. All continuities are refused. Nor is
reading it a straightforward matter as it isn't always clear
where to begin or end. It reads like an ululation, like some-

thing primordial, page after page of elusive meaning. In the afterword Philip tells us that the words in *Zong!* come from a 1783 British legal report on *Gregson v. Gilbert.* The Messrs. Gregson were the owners of the *Zong,* the Messrs. Gilbert its underwriters. This report, of a decision by three justices of the Court of King's Bench, came after an appeal of an earlier judgment that had found the insurers liable for the loss of the one hundred and fifty Africans who had been forced to their deaths by Captain Collingwood. Presiding over the Court of King's Bench on the occasion of the decision relayed in the report was Lord Mansfield, the Lord Chief Justice of England.

And it is this language of law, this formal, allegedly objective, allegedly neutral language, that Philip fashions into *Zong!* She makes the legal language into something incantatory, distressed, and oneiric. She wanted to lock herself, she writes, in the "word store" of the legal text. The original text addresses a dispute between an insurer and a merchant and in that original text there's no suggestion that this was a profit-driven mass murder of human beings, that these murdered Africans were human. And yet Lord Mansfield should have and would have known better, for he raised his nephew's daughter, a half-black girl named Dido, as a lady in his own household. For Dido's sake Lord Mansfield could not have been in doubt about black humanity. But when a man's existential satisfaction depends on not knowing something he very much will find a way to not know it.

By using the words of that already foul legal text, by shearing some of those words, by going on a rampage inside that locked word store, Philip wails out the lives of the people massacred on the *Zong*. Like Turner she paints a picture of a creaking ship beset by heaving waves. But out of that ragged material she has made something far more personal and holy. We get a sense of actual persons destroyed. We are spattered by history's bitter spray. It is not the spectacle of loss that Philip foregrounds but rather the interwoven hurt of these people, not impossible limbs as painted by Turner but possible lives taken from people for whom, in the absence of records, she has conjured credible names: Muru, Kakra, Kolawole, Kibibi, Olabisi, Usi, Kenyatta, Mesi, Nayo, Yooku, Ngena, Wale, Sade, Ade.

THE SUN SETS IN *Slavers Throwing Overboard the Dead and Dying* as it sets every day. Blazing as its colors are, the sky it depicts is not literally on fire. But I turn now to another painting in the collection of this museum, smaller and much less well-known, which features a similarly livid sky. Farther back in time from Turner's painting than Turner's painting is from us, *Landscape with Burning City* is thought to have been painted around 1500 by the Flemish master Herri met de Bles. The scholarship on Bles is insecure. For instance, his date of birth can differ from one scholarly source to another by up to twenty-five years. His family name is unknown; "met de Bles" means "with the white forelock" or "with the blaze," a description of his distinctive hair. But he is believed to have been born in Bouvignes or Dinant and to have been the nephew of Joachim Patinir, one of the first great innovators in the so-called world-landscape tradition. The mastery of a moody atmospheric perspective in which blue and green predominate in the far distance certainly links Bles with Patinir.

Those cool colors sit side by side with the hot ones in *Landscape with Burning City*, a painting some ten inches across, only about a fifth as wide as *Slavers Throwing Overboard the Dead and Dying*.

Bles's compact painting is busy with detail. The redness in the sky is from burning buildings on two headlands jutting into a port. In the middle distance are two ships, one of which seems to have run aground, the other listing perilously in shallow water. In the far distance are other ships, a townscape with numerous fires, and the soaring steeple of a cathedral. At the upper left of the panel are those vertiginous mountains that were as common in Flemish landscape paintings as they were impossible to find in the flat terrain of Flanders itself. The dark and muddy foreground is riven by a winding path but is meticulously painted with carefully rendered rocks and stippled foliage. In that foreground is a single person in a blue robe and a white turban, probably a biblical personage, who stands underneath a solitary tree of deep green. The winding path leads the eye via a low wooden gate back towards the burning port.

There is in this little painting both something of hell and of an escape from it. Perhaps it suggests Abraham's unsuccessful bargaining with God for the sparing of Sodom and Gomorrah. Or perhaps it depicts Lot and his wife and what looks like a dry stump behind the leafy tree is a pillar of salt discolored by time. Possibly the panel was simply painted to satisfy a client's wish for a city undergoing destruction. Hellscapes, in addition to cityscapes, seascapes, and mountain views, were part of the surging Netherlandish interest in dramatic panoramic views. The world is a wild and wondrous place, it cannot be mastered, but within the dimensions of a painted picture, large or small, some of its complexity can be contemplated and some of its strangeness can be enjoyed. This world-landscape tradition may well have had its beginnings in the elegant and understated backgrounds of portraits by Hans Memling in the final quarter of the fifteenth century which so influenced Italian portraitists in the generation after him but which in his native Netherlands would soar to weird and impressive heights in the works of Patinir and Hieronymus Bosch. A century after Memling this commitment to landscape painting persisted in the celebrated oeuvres of Lucas van Valckenborch, Hendrick van Cleve III, Paul Bril, and above all Pieter Bruegel the Elder, a company of impressive names in which Herri met de Bles is a minor master.

Bles's surviving works have a brooding and haunted character conveyed by his immense skill at simultaneously depicting obsessive detail and the evanescent look of great distances, a skill at which he surpassed some of his esteemed contemporaries, among them Lucas Gassel and the Master LC. But the haunting is there too in his peculiar habit of painting an inconspicuous little owl somewhere in each of his panels. It was this mysterious avian signature that led the Italians, when he moved to their country late in his career, to give him the byname "il Civetta," the little owl. I have been unable to detect an owl in *Landscape with Burning City*, though I do not doubt the attribution to Bles. The assigned date of 1500 does seem early: there is documentation listing Bles as a free master in Antwerp in 1535 and several paintings attributed to him from as late as the 1540s are recognizably in the style of *Landscape with Burning City*, a great span of time for an unwavering technique. Art historians have been examining the evidence for centuries and no fully satisfactory timeline has yet emerged for Bles. But perhaps the most curious aspect of this intense little panel—a panel that is somehow both as quiet as a mist and as loud as a conflagration—is the history that has brought it to rest, for now, within the walls of this museum.

Let us move some four centuries beyond the making of the painting. Bear with me, what follows is slightly tangled. Around 1929 *Landscape with Burning City* was owned by Franz W. Koenigs, a German Protestant who lived in Haarlem. Koenigs was a businessman and in 1931 he took out a loan from the Dutch bank Lisser & Rosenkranz using his art collection as collateral. The agreement was formalized in 1935 and payment was understood to be due five years later in 1940. If Koenigs was unable to pay the loan when it came due or if the Lisser & Rosenkranz bank was liquidated before the five-year term was up the bank would have the right to sell the collection. A summary of these events is publicly available in the Museum of Fine Arts' provenance note for *Landscape with Burning City*. By April 1940 it was evident that Koenigs did not have the means to repay his loan. Furthermore Lisser & Rosenkranz did go into liquidation and so, according to the terms of the loan agreement, they were allowed to sell Koenigs's paintings. The bank engaged the services of the prominent Amsterdam art dealer Jacques Goudstikker to help with the sale. In April 1940 Jacques Goudstikker took thirty-five paintings from the Koenigs collection. The provenance note does not mention that on May 14, the day that the Luftwaffe bombed Rotterdam into submission, killing some nine hundred residents of that city, Goudstikker himself, who was Jewish, fled Amsterdam for England along with his family on board the SS *Bodegraven*. On the darkened steamship the following day Goudstikker accidentally stepped into a hatch and plunging downwards broke his neck and died. He was forty-two years old.

On the same day Goudstikker died, the day of the Dutch surrender, before the bodies were cold, so to speak, a certain Alois Miedl—and this is now back to the provenance note— a German banker based in the Netherlands, visited the Goudstikker gallery. The gallery was now run by Jacques Goudstikker's employees and Miedl's visit was made in the company of a certain eminent person. The following month, June 1940, Miedl purchased from the Goudstikker gallery thirty-one paintings that had originated from Koenigs's collection, including *Landscape with Burning City*, allegedly with the active participation of Franz Koenigs. (Koenigs himself was to die the following year in Cologne, falling in front of a train from the platform; his descendants believe he was murdered by Nazis.) On the same month in which he bought the paintings Miedl sold nineteen of them, again including *Landscape with Burning City*, to the man who had accompanied him some weeks earlier to Goudstikker's gallery. That buyer was the supreme commander of the Luftwaffe, Hitler's second-in-command, Hermann Göring. The paintings arrived at Carinhall, Göring's palace in the Berlin suburb of Templin, on June 10.

We do not know where exactly in the sumptuous interior of Carinhall *Landscape with Burning City* was displayed. Possibly it was in the monumental skylit Festhalle alongside hundreds of other works or perhaps it was in the great vaulted library. Or perhaps on account of its small scale, its intimate scale that invites up-close contemplation, it was in one of the smaller rooms: the music room, a bedroom, or Göring's own private study. When we rest our eyes on the subtle atmospheric effects achieved by Bles we imagine that at quiet moments the Reichsmarschall Hermann Göring did the same, that from time to time over a period of five years, seeking refuge from the hell he had helped create, he rested his eyes on the blues and greens blended on the panel by il Civetta. Or perhaps he never did. Göring's taste was flamboyant and he had a preference for large fleshy nudes. Perhaps he bought the Bles painting and promptly forgot about it. We cannot know. His collection was full of substandard works as well as a number of fakes including a "Vermeer" painted by the Dutch master forger van Meegeren. Carinhall was testament more to acquisitiveness than to connoisseurship.

Outside, the war went on. Death with its big heavy boots was trampling everything. Göring, as Hitler's number two, was profoundly involved in massacres all over Europe, in the looting of Jewish property, and in the planning and undertaking of the Holocaust. Göring's haul of paintings is but a small part of the cultural genocide aspect of the unspeakable crimes in which he was involved. He did his collecting with an extensive network of agents and enablers all over Europe, men like Alois Miedl who had taken control of Goudstikker's gallery, men like Walter Andreas Hofer, Kurt von Behr, and Bruno Lohse, men who dragged in at any cost, sometimes paying too much and sometimes paying nothing at all, paint-

ings by Rubens, Titian, Cranach, men who acquired tapes-
tries, sculptures, and plate from France, Poland, Italy, the
Low Countries, and elsewhere.

I remember now a striking scene in James Ivory's 1993
film adaptation of Kazuo Ishiguro's *The Remains of the Day*,
an episode that Ivory dramatizes for the film but which does
not occur in the book. While waiting before dinner in a ro-
tunda at the fictional Darlington Hall the German ambassador Joachim von Ribbentrop and two of his attachés inspect
the paintings and porcelains in the room with quietly ravenous eyes. One of the attachés leans forward towards a large
picture in a gilded frame and says, "Herri met de Bles painted
this. Sixteenth century." I have always remembered the scene
because one does not hear Bles's name often. The other at-
taché draws Ribbentrop's attention to the painting and Ribbentrop ominously tells him to "note it down for later."

The war approached its end. The wreckage to humanity
and to all human decency was incalculable. In early 1945, to
safeguard his Carinhall collection Göring attempted to send
it by train to another of his properties, his villa in Berchtesgaden in Bavaria.

I am sorry. I'm so sorry.

Gosh. Pardon the interruption. Strange as it might sound
I've just had a medical episode. For about thirty seconds just
now I lost vision in one of my eyes. But please don't be
alarmed: it's a transient incident. It should be transient. It
happens to me only once in a great while. Sorry about this, it

took me by surprise this time. But I think I'm OK now. The vision is coming back and I think it's best if I press on.

Yes I'm sure. I'll continue.

So, yes, "note it down for later." To safeguard his Carinhall collection Göring attempted to send it by train to another of his properties, his villa in Berchtesgaden in Bavaria. But the train was intercepted by Allied troops and a substantial part of the collection was officially recovered. A large number of items were looted after the interception, by locals, by American soldiers, and by other Allied troops. *Landscape with Burning City*, small and easy to steal, went missing at this time. It vanished in the fog of war. Many of the other objects that had originated from Goudstikker's gallery were returned to the Netherlands where they became property of the Dutch government. In 1946, a year after Göring killed himself with cyanide pills at Nuremberg, the Museum of Fine Arts purchased *Landscape with Burning City*. The MFA bought the painting from Aram Gallery in New York City. Siegfried Aram claimed to have acquired the painting from a New York restorer named Julian Acampora. Acampora obtained the painting from unclear sources: there are mentions of the Count d'Urbania, of Devany's auction galleries, of "a collection in Chicago." What seems clear is that the work was looted, sold on the black market, and ended up here.

The provenance note goes on to say that as early as 1948 the Museum of Fine Arts was aware of the painting's previous ownership and of the Dutch claim to such works. At the museum's invitation the matter was turned over to the General Commission of Recuperation in Amsterdam but the Dutch did not follow up the matter. Fifty years later, in 1998, perhaps with the new focus in the art world on questions of Nazi loot and restitution the museum corresponded again with the Dutch state, this time through the Inspectorate of Cultural Heritage, and it was confirmed that the Dutch believed they had a legitimate claim to the painting. Two complications soon attended their assertion. One was a suit by the heirs of the gallerist Jacques Goudstikker over the paintings that had been sold to Miedl. That case was settled in 1999 with a court ruling against the Goudstikker heirs. The second was a claim brought by an heir of Franz Koenigs who asserted that Koenigs had been forced to sell his collection at prices well below market value. Given the circumstances of Goudstikker's flight and his accidental death—not to mention Göring's involvement as an eventual owner—this is well within the realm of possibility. But the Dutch Advisory Committee on the Assessment of Restitution Applications rejected the claim in 2003.

The status, then, of *Landscape with Burning City* is complex and for many years the painting has not been on view in Boston. It sits at this very moment behind these walls. What is perhaps most striking to me is the apparent good faith effort by the museum, perhaps in recognition of the horrific circumstance through which the painting was obtained, to let go of it if and when the legal mechanism for doing so presents itself. The provenance note ends as follows: "The MFA awaits communication from the interested parties regarding their attempts to reach a neutral resolution of the ownership of the painting." And it is this phrase I would like to hold on to, it is this phrase that I would like to "note down for later": the MFA awaits communication from the interested parties.

THE BOOK OF EVENTS is always open in the middle. In February 1897 a British army approached first the outlying villages and then the immense city of Benin itself on the coast of West Africa. The Niger Coast Protectorate and Admiralty forces came by sea and creek and forest. Earlier a British expedition had been cut off at the pass on the orders of some Benin chiefs. Before that an aggressive treaty imposed by the Royal Niger Company, a treaty that amounted to subjugation, had been rejected by the Oba of Benin. Now the British army, some fourteen hundred strong, was approaching, bristling with modern weaponry and intent on vengeance. They were not there to negotiate. They came armed with mountain guns, bolt-action rifles, rocket tubes and war rockets, and, above all, fourteen rapid-firing Maxim guns. They descended on Benin like hellfire and began killing right away. There was no official accounting of the death toll during the resulting massacre. Historians have had to estimate the number of people killed in Benin during the eighteen-day attack by using a terrifying metric: the number of rounds fired from the British guns. Eyewitnesses report seeing hundreds of bodies cut to pieces in the dense forests near the city.

Who shall we say these massacred people were? I think it is important to try to imagine them as real and individual people. Imagine that you are Bini and have survived the massacre and the news of who didn't survive begins to reach you. The most famous wrestler in the empire is dead. The head of the market women's guild is dead. Her best friend, the one with the marvelously musical laugh, is dead too. The girl with the red ribbon in her hair is dead. The boy with perfect pitch is dead, as is his shy and handsome younger brother. The sculptor whose leg was taken in his youth by a crocodile is dead. The agile elder who thatched roofs and never once lost his balance is dead. The youth with inscrutable eyes and a raging inner life is dead. The identical twins with the ironic smiles, the man with the elegant neck: this is death's kingdom now. Male and female, young and old, they lie in pools of dark blood over a vast terrain, in pools of silence. The British have fired four million rounds, besides the use of fires, mines, and rockets. Why did the British murder all these people? In the aftermath, the high chiefs are singled out and hanged in the marketplace. The Oba himself, Ovonramwen Nogbaisi, is exiled, never to return.

The killing done, the looting begins. The assault on Benin now became an attempt at cultural obliteration. The great city was stripped of its material glory, in particular its works of ritual and artistic significance. Buildings were burned, sacred places desecrated, and palaces destroyed. Methodically centuries of ivory carvings and of metal plaques and metal sculptures were carted away. The metal sculptures were made of brass and other copper alloys though they are often simply called bronzes. Magnificent heads of Bini obas, high chiefs, and deified ancestors were piled up and shipped out by British soldiers. No fewer than four thousand objects were expropriated from destroyed Benin and scattered across the world, ostensibly to pay for the cost of the invasion. The material heritage of Bini people became a core component of the ethnographic art that filled the storerooms and displays of museums in places like London, Oxford, Cambridge, Berlin, Vienna, Philadelphia, New York, Edinburgh, Dublin, Vancouver, Basel, Washington, D.C., Glasgow, Cleveland, Liverpool, and Boston.

Let us contemplate an object such as this one: a copper-alloy relief plaque showing three courtiers playing musical instruments. All three face us frontally. The figure in the middle, larger than the other two and more elaborately dressed with latticed beadwork on his headwear and geometrical patterns on his robes, plays a drum with his flattened palms. The figures flanking him echo each other, from the gongs they hold with their left hands and strike with their right to the slight rightward inclination of their helmeted heads. The artist has paid particular attention in this bas-relief to the upper and lower eyelids of each figure and to their broad flared noses. With the abundance of decorative detail on all three bodies and the floral motifs in the background, the dark, burnished plaque summons up an entire world of West African experience, a world of artists, patrons, guilds, iconography, and critical practice. Yes, critical practice, because wherever it is that we encounter excellence in the visual arts, there is implied a critical apparatus for evaluating the success of those individual artworks in comparison to others from the same context.

This impressive plaque is one of thirty-two from Benin currently in the collection of this museum. It is on view in a small gallery here which many of you will no doubt have visited. The plaque is estimated to have been made between 1530 and 1570 by the Benin guild of bronze casters during the

reigns of Oba Esigie and his son and successor Oba Orhog-
bua. It would have been one of hundreds attached to the pil-
lars of a courtyard in the royal palace. Such images presented
Benin's history to the people of the kingdom. They were the
visual record of its kings and gods.

I am struck by a coincidence in both the subject and the
dates of this particular plaque with a small grisaille painting
on oak panel by Pieter Bruegel the Elder. The Bruegel painting, titled *Three Soldiers,* is thought to have been made in
1568. Like the Benin plaque it is a work of modest size and it
too depicts musician-soldiers full-length in ceremonial rega-
lia. One of Bruegel's soldiers plays a flute, a motif also seen
in Benin plaques. In such mysterious ways do synchronicities
occur across vast distances, as though one person's two hands
were simultaneously drawing two images from a single
model. The soldiers in this plaque wear coral beads around
their faces, symbolic of dignity, and their cloth wrappers are
fastened into place with large brooches in the form of a leopard's face, the leopard being the symbol of the Oba's tenac-
ity, strength, and cunning.

But whatever visual pleasures plaques such as this might
offer there is an act of violent displacement behind them that
we have a responsibility to consider. There's a story here that
cannot be told, as M. NourbeSe Philip writes of the *Zong,*
and we must tell it. The Benin plaque is no mere work of art
but rather the residue of a vast cultural experience that is now
decontextualized. It was removed from its proper place in the
aftermath of a mass killing, amid the stench of human bodies.
It emerged from a landscape with a burning city. To describe
it as being part of the "Robert Owen Lehman Collection"—

to center its history on its having been purchased at auction by a wealthy American—is to suppress the plain truth of why such a thing is in other people's keeping. To speak even of a "punitive expedition," as is commonly done in the literature on Benin, is to accept the British version: that vengeance for the deaths of five or seven white men justified the destruction of the life-worlds of hundreds of thousands of people. It is to tacitly accept that the mission to "civilize" Benin was worth the destruction of Benin's civilization and the mass murder of its people.

Our education—I mean the kind of university education many of us here today have—has encouraged us to think of art as something requiring great care. We know not to touch objects in museums. We are all obsessed with preservation and we revere scholarship and curation. But we have not been concurrently taught to value the life-worlds of others, their autonomy, their ancestral rights. Particularly if the people in question are from the African continent, their ingenuity can be appreciated, their artifacts can be acquired and subjected to analysis, but their actual lives cannot be valued. What does it mean to care about art but not about the people who made that art? And this brings me again to the annotation I found so memorable in the provenance note about Herri met de Bles's painting: that "the MFA awaits communication from the interested parties." No such invitation is appended to the provenance descriptions of the Benin works currently held in this museum. It is as though certain things might legitimately be discussed and certain others might never be thought worthy of such consideration.

As I have said the shock for me is unabating each time I

encounter Turner's *Slavers Throwing Overboard the Dead and Dying*. But of late I have begun to experience the museum itself as a zone of sustained shocks. These are shocks that issue out of a feeling of moral whiplash: the meticulousness of curatorial practice on the one hand and those dark pools of human blood on the other. The Benin works contain a plea and their plea is not isolated. It is shared by other works in this museum, works "acquired" from Kuba, Sébé, Mandé, Hemba, Mangbetu, and Yoruba people, among others. It is a plea to rethink the idea that Western understanding surpasses that of the people who made and sacralized these objects, that aesthetic appreciation or critical practice exists only here. It is a plea to take restitution seriously, a plea to reimagine the future of the museum, to reimagine it not as a space of superior knowledge or as a storehouse of other people's stolen worlds but as a place of inflection in which new conversations about justice might be possible. The museum in other words has for a long time loved other people's objects with a death grip. Can it surrender that deadly love? Afterwards new loves might bloom, new possibilities might emerge. If we go down that path the contents of this building will be different in the future and our collective understanding of the ownership of historically significant artworks might change. But I want to suggest that this change is not something to be feared.

BEAR WITH ME AS I come to the end now. I am alert to the feeling of discomfort that might go through people who describe themselves as lovers of art when they hear such suggestions. Indeed, following another talk I gave, I had a thoughtful gentleman suggest to me during the question-and-answer period that restitution was all well and good but the reality was that certain cultures were not able to take good care of their own artifacts. What were we to do then? I appreciated his directness. He gave the not-unreasonable example of the destruction of the monumental Buddhas in the Bamiyan Valley in early 2001. Would it not be safer, this man suggested, to remove works of universal importance from cultures that were, in his words, "less able to care for them"? After pausing for thought I responded to him by saying that in the first instance a sandstone Buddha fifty-five meters high and carved into a cliff would not have been movable. We are all vulnerable to the madnesses of history. But more important, I said, his proposal was based on two assumptions. One was about people and institutions in places he didn't know, about the forms of expertise and attentiveness present in those places and appropriate to the needs there. The other assumption was that the West was impeccable or even reliable in its record of the care of artworks. And yet it was the Allied forces who in their 1945 attack on Magdeburg destroyed Vincent van Gogh's *The Painter on the Road to Tarascon*, a work of universal importance. It was they who incinerated during their firebombing of Dresden in the same year Gustave Courbet's *The Stone Breakers*, a work of universal importance. And when the Flakturm Friedrichshain in Berlin went up in flames in the final year of the war more than a hundred paintings were lost for all time among them masterworks by Ghirlandaio, Murillo, Rubens, Titian, Goya, Botticelli, Tintoretto, and Caravaggio. It is a melancholy exercise to look at faded pre-war photographs of some of those paintings now. No one will ever stand before Caravaggio's *Saint Matthew and the Angel* again, no one will ever be consoled by that extraordinary painting's agony and sensuality, by its sublime doubt. I cannot help but think, I said to my interlocutor at that event, that these irreplaceable treasures would be with us now if only they had been kept somewhere truly safe during the Second World War. Somewhere like Lagos for instance.

But later, I must say, I felt guilty about the asymmetry of the question-and-answer format. After all, the audience on that occasion as on this one had come to see me talk and this questioner was already at a disadvantage. I had a microphone and he didn't. He was given no right of response. My answer, accurate though it might have been, also had an air of showmanship to it. So immediate, sharp, and factual was my response that the audience applauded and in fact cheered my answer. It was as though there had been a combat and I had triumphed. I was embarrassed. If I were asked to respond to that man again I think I would be more succinct. Perhaps I would respond to him only by citing the German incendiary bomb that hit the Liverpool Museum in May 1941. That bomb and the resulting fire led to the destruction of thousands of artifacts gathered from around the world many of which had been acquired through colonial violence. Among those destroyed objects was a brass head of the Queen Mother, the Iyoba, looted from Benin in 1897. Perhaps I would have said to him that any ethics that persistently considered works of art more valuable than human life was no ethics at all. Perhaps I could have done a better job of persuading him that my point was not to give a brilliant retort but to convey my genuine sorrow at the long and persistent history of white people thinking they know better than the rest of us. That, I think, would be a good place to stop. Thank you all for your attention tonight.

SIX

We were crossing Third Mainland Bridge when they began to play some old music on the radio. There was sudden excitement in my boss's voice and he asked me to turn up the volume. This is Fela, he said, how can you not know Fela? This is "Water No Get Enemy." Then he started to talk about the music, about how it was this, how it was that. I have come to recognize that excitement in his voice, an excitement that reminds me of how far apart our lives are. When I hear it I want to tell him to come to Ifako Agege where I live, where we line up for water from the borehole at the baale's house and pay five hundred naira for two jerry cans of water. Every day fights break out on that long line of jerry cans and buckets. I have a younger brother who hasn't walked normally since some thugs beat him up on the water line two years ago. And sometimes when there is no electricity and the baale doesn't want to pump with his generator there is no water at all. The whole neighborhood goes without. I don't even think the government knows we exist. Meanwhile at his own house my boss opens the tap and water comes out. Water is not *his* enemy. Please I am not saying this to complain. I'm sure you understand.

I have been driving cautiously since yesterday because the horn in this car is out. Lagos drivers are very aggressive. I can hear them coming but they can't hear me. Without a horn I am like someone without a voice. This is not just an inconvenience, it is extremely dangerous. If I have an accident and I damage the car Oga Tomi will release me from the job. If I get injured and end up in hospital my savings will be wiped out. Those are the things that make it hard to share his enjoyment of music. But I still laugh when I'm supposed to laugh and I smile when I am supposed to smile.

Each day when we get home he gives me an extra thousand naira. "Nestor, take this." That's how he says it. The amount is nothing to him. I see the places where he stops for lunch. I have helped him price leather goods at the market. It isn't easy to hide your spending habits from your driver in this city where I am your eyes more than your own eyes. I am not complaining about the tip: the one thousand naira almost doubles what else I earn from my salary for the day. But I also know that if he is in a certain mood, if something has irritated him whether or not it's my fault, he only gives me five hundred. I am probably saying too much. Sometimes my tip is nothing just because he's tired and can't be bothered to search his bag. Should I be grateful? There are many people in this city who would take my job tomorrow. I am very grateful.

I CAME IN FROM Okota this morning. Traffic to the island was hell. A tanker broke down in Oshodi and everything just stopped. This was at 7:00 A.M. We were just there for an hour, nothing moving. One thing this city can do is waste your time. It was past 9:00 when we arrived at Igbosere and when we arrived we arrived only to wait. There was a row of seats in the hall. We sat leaning forward so that our heads wouldn't rest on the greasy circles left on the wall by other heads. They finally called us in and I heard Okanlawon continue his testimony. The man is full of nonsense. Week after week I have returned to the courtroom and listened to his big grammar. All I am interested in is my three million naira. Where is it? I am a serious person and I don't like to be emotional in public but everyone has a limit. That is why I raised my voice in the courtroom. Maybe this is what people think of when they think of a market woman, as someone who has no self-control. But ask Kehinde and she will tell you. I am one of the most controlled people you will ever meet. *Alara tutu ni mi.*

Okanlawon is my brother. Let him be my brother. That does not mean he can sell our father's property without giving me my fair share. Is it because I am a woman? Am I not the same woman who runs her own electronics shop? Am I not the same woman who cooked his meals when he was a child? I presented the court with text messages between us, a handwritten letter from him, statements from my bank account. The court also made him show his bank statements. Now they have adjourned again. What more do they need to know?

I'll be honest with you, this thing has been a struggle. If not for the way we don't go gray in my family my hair would be gray by now. I give Kehinde credit. She has been with me from the beginning of the case. We understand each other woman to woman. So when she said she wanted to bring her brother to the courtroom I said bring him. It doesn't matter that I dislike my own brother. Do I look tired to you? Do I look like someone who gives up easily? Let

them adjourn, let them keep adjourning, I will collect my
money. Being fifty-two years old is not a joke and being a
woman is not an offense. One thing I have learned is that if
you don't know how to wait you're not ready for this Lagos.

IN THE EARLY NINETIES I was friends with one Mr. Ejigboye.
You wouldn't know the name, he was not prominent, but he
and I undertook a business venture together. It was a development deal, the kind of thing I didn't know anything about
back then. But I was having difficulties with the factory and
had my eye out for any opportunity. Ejigboye was someone
I trusted. We were to be given one hundred and fifty thousand naira to refurbish some government housing units.
This was a lot of money back then, worth forty times more
than the same amount today. The contract was for a hundred and fifty thousand and the first installment was fifty
thousand naira, about five thousand dollars back then. Ejigboye was a developer but I was the one who knew someone
in government. Her name escapes me at the moment, some
double-barreled name.

Anyway this was why we were in business together: I
had the contacts, he had the know-how. And even though it
is not the kind of thing a person should say out loud, people
often want to have a Lebanese business partner. It gives
them legitimacy. So I knew that was part of my role. The
fact that I presented Ejigboye was a seal of approval. Of
that first installment sixteen thousand naira went to kickbacks, some directly to the woman I knew in government.

That left thirty-four thousand all of which I gave to Ejigboye to execute the contract. Everything was fine up to that
point. But then Ejigboye began to act strange. Nigeria is my
home and I am not prejudiced against Nigerians. I myself
am a Nigerian. If someone says to me that Yoruba people
are this or Igbo people are that I make it clear I don't like to
be around that kind of talk. I don't tolerate tribalism. But I
have to say that around that time my head started to fill with
imaginings. Ejigboye missed some meetings, then he
stopped answering my calls and it finally dawned on me that
yes once again, this being Lagos, the man had simply taken
the money and walked. It is the oldest story. It makes you
humble. You think it can't be you, you think you cannot be
the victim of fraud until you wake up one day and guess
what.

I had to go to the woman I knew in government,
Mrs. Bello-Clark. That's her name, it just came back to me.
Bello-Clark. It was a painful incident. I was naive about
these things and it was the time I felt most like a foreigner
here. I got scammed like any foreigner would though I was
born and raised here. But the thing with scammers is that
they think they're cleverer than God and they are not.
Guess what I heard last week? The man had died, Mr. Ejigboye. You can't take it with you. We heard he died, liver
cancer or something like that it seems.

I DECIDED TO BECOME a woman at the age of twenty-one. I
mean I have always been a woman and I was assigned fe-

male at birth. But when I turned twenty-one I became a woman in a more conscious way. I found that I had to learn to walk like a woman, like what society thought of as a woman. At some point I just realized that *not* learning it was too much work and then I found out that I was good at it. Our culture has rigid ideas of what a woman is and what a man is but I've always been a free person and the cost of my freedom is that it took me time to figure out how to move in this society. I mean how to move in my interactions but I also mean how to move in my body. I don't think of this as transgressive. The way I walked before did not transgress anything and beginning to walk like a woman didn't either. When we really talk about transgression that's something that is addressing other people and challenging their opinion. But I did it for myself, I am doing it for myself. I am the one I am addressing.

You have to know how to move in Lagos in all the senses of moving. I'll give you an example. Not long after I left university a friend took me to a small gathering which I thought was going to be at someone's house but it turned out to be at a private club in V.I. Among certain kinds of men in this city, men with money, there is wives' night and there is girlfriends' night. So I'm at this private club in V.I. and as the night winds down two of the women leave. Then my friend who has to get back to Yaba leaves and another man leaves with another woman. Suddenly I asked myself what I was doing there. No one had said anything to me or offered me anything. But I looked around and realized that I was surrounded by men, only men, and all of them owned private jets. You suddenly wake up to your life in the middle of some night and find yourself saying: what the hell am I doing here?

What you want is situations you have chosen for yourself. What looks like control is dangerous and what looks like giving up control can be where you are most powerful. I'll give you another example. Recently I met a man who had a serious interest in hiking. The moment he said so I knew he would have other "interests" as well. And I was right: he was into BDSM. Now I'm someone who is willing to try anything once, so when the relationship progressed in the sexual direction and he asked me if I would be willing to be submissive I agreed. The ground rules were that I consented to being rough-handled by him. If he hits me it's part of the game. If he strikes me it's part of the game. Yes, I said, fine, fine. I wasn't about to let hiker boy out-freak me.

Anyway the first time we get down to business he smacks me playfully on the ass. Then he smacks me less playfully. We are there, nothing exists but the game, I am on top of him, riding him, I am lost in it. This goes on for a while. He continues to hit me and the hitting becomes harder. Am I enjoying this aspect of it? I don't know. Then he slaps me on the face and in that moment I completely forget the game. I slap him back very swiftly, very hard. Who the hell are you! I still can't tell the story without laughing. The look of shock on his face was so extreme that I had to begin to beg him. I was afraid I'd knocked a tooth out of his mouth. I guess my inner Yoruba woman came out. Don't slap me man! Anyway that was the last time we had sex. I'm still laughing about it, God forgive me. In fact that was the last time I saw him.

———

WHEN THE CRISIS WAS really bad we used to go to LUTH. But what could they do? We just sat there for hours among other people with their own issues, people with wounds you could see and wounds you couldn't see. A hospital day was a day I couldn't go to work. I have a job as a sweeper at a crèche in Ilupeju, a twenty-thousand-naira job, and things got to the point where they were saying they would lay me off. But I could not let the fear of the job keep me from taking care of my child. The father had gone abroad but he had left us even before going abroad. My daughter and I only had each other.

By the end she became so small. Her eyes got bigger and yellower. She was fourteen years old but no one who saw her would believe it. The crises got worse. Sometimes they lasted up to three days. We stayed in our one room and I would beg her to eat, and I would give her pure water to drink. I cooked moin-moin for her. I made it very soft but even that was difficult for her to swallow. Her legs became swollen and her fingers were cold. Sometimes she refused Panadol when the pain of swallowing became too much. I did not bring a child into this world only to watch her suffer like this. I don't understand again.

When she died I held her in my arms and cried. I wanted to cry with my whole chest but I had to be conscious of the neighbors. So I was crying and holding the crying in at the same time. In the morning I called her father's people. I told the father's older brother I needed money for the arrangements and he said he would come but only the following week. I didn't have money for the mortuary which is fifty thousand weekly. Where was I going to find that kind of money? The girl's body was just there in our room. I covered her with my wrapper and closed the windows.

I talked to Iya Ramota about it and she advised me to go to Celina Pharmacy and ask for the formalin. She said the bigger pharmacies would not agree to sell it to me because it is against the law. So I went and I paid the five thousand and they gave me the syringe and the formalin. That was how I managed to preserve the body for some days before I could make the funeral arrangements. The man at the pharmacy had said if I couldn't find the blood vessel to put the syringe into I should pour the formalin into my daughter's mouth, nose, and privates and block everything with cotton wool. But I knew I would find the blood vessel. I took this girl to hospital so many times. I knew her body like I know my own. Sometimes I was the one who put the drip on her. I was the one who gave her injections. The only thing that changed was that when I inserted the needle for the last time she did not feel any pain. My daughter's name was Durotola. It means "stay with glory."

MY MOTHER WAS EASYGOING. She respected her religion but she was a calm person about it. But her father whom I knew when I was a child was anything but easygoing. He was known for his sternness and extreme Islamic belief. If he were alive today he'd be the kind of person you could compare to Boko Haram. His trousers never reached the ground and he was skeptical of Western education and bicycles and sewing machines. He was an imam, your great-grandfather. He died long before you were born though your great-grandmother lived until you were about ten. His name was Waleed and his father, named Hamzat, was also an imam. Hamzat was in fact the first imam in Amu Ewa. This would have been in the last two decades of the nineteenth century. There are no photographs of either of them.

Hamzat's father was Esude. It is a rare name: "Esu has arrived." Between the generation of Esude and his son, Islamic religion came to our people. Hamzat would have been an early convert, probably under the influence of preachers from the north, from Ilorin and Hausaland. That's where Islam came in from, usually into areas that at the same time were also resisting Christianity. Missionaries feared Ijebu people and Remo people. They say we were especially stubborn and wicked. Esude was a blacksmith and his name makes me think he was also involved in the priesthood of Esu or his family was. I don't know when that might have been, maybe around the middle of the nineteenth century. I imagine him holding on to the traditional truths while all around him everyone was finally converting.

Anyway it goes without saying that we don't believe in Esu anymore. We would probably have said back then that Esu is the god of interpretation and also of mischief, that he is the one who spins messages around and sets people against each other. But as Christians we learned more and came to believe that Esu is the same as Satan or the Devil. That is why *isé Esu* is now the way we describe evil: "the Devil's works."

When I married your dad and became a Christian you could say that it was like that change from Esude to Hamzat.

You could say it's that kind of change, a dramatic change where the world is completely altered. I actually now never think of when I was a Muslim. We have to know how to forget the past in order to make progress into the future. Some people did traditional religion and some did Islam and some did Christianity. That is how eyes gradually open. Whenever a person wakes up, that is morning for them. But this *your* thing of not believing anything at all, I don't see that as progress. A person has to believe something.

IT WAS NOT AN ordinary job. First of all the institution had boarders as well as day students like yourself so you can imagine all the complexities involved in the procurement of food, the repair of facilities, the operation of the school health clinic, and so on. These were complex things and as I found out as soon as I joined the school the complexity was a breeding ground for all kinds of corruption. There were bribes, kickbacks, what have you. When I began and let them know that I was putting a stop to all that, people said this woman is crazy. I would just smile and say if you come to offer me a bribe that contract you've been enjoying will be given to somebody else.

The other thing about the role was that GCS in those days improved rapidly and was thought of as being one of the most prestigious government high schools. I turned the place around in six months. The SSCE results were fantastic, the JAMB results were among the best in the nation and suddenly everyone wanted their children to go there. They were choosing us over King's College and Queen's College.

People were saying who's this Laseinde woman? Within a
few years I had not only brilliant students but also the children of the high and mighty who, it will come as no surprise
to you, were not always brilliant students. So that was the
other thing about the job: it was very political. I was like a
political appointee. But somehow I knew my way around.

One day the wife of the military governor of the state
came to see her son. The boy must have been some years junior to you. Remember that the governor at that time was
nicknamed Hitler. His name was Brigadier Okon but everyone called him Hitler. So Hitler's wife shows up and says
she wants to see her son. And I said I'm sorry madam but
visits are not allowed outside visiting hours, we cannot
make special concessions for anybody. You can imagine the
rage that followed. But I refused to let her see her son. What
did this woman not say to me that day? And I thought to
myself, my God I am really going to lose this job.

Three days later as I feared Hitler himself came into the
school. He and his aide-de-camp sat in my office. I was
shaking of course but I was also really respectful. Welcome
sir, coffee sir? While I'm brewing the coffee, he says, as if
he's just making conversation: there's a JS3 student here,
Hezekiah Okon. He's my son. I'd like to see him. So what
do I say in response to that? I say: of course sir, I'll have
him summoned right away! I call in my deputy principal and
ask him to go pull young Master Hezekiah from his classes.
The logic is clear in my head: Hitler's wife is not my boss
but as a government employee I am under the command of
the state governor. It was like a military order not a request
from a parent.

But this is why I agree with those who say I'm a crazy woman. Because while Hitler and the aide-de-camp were drinking their coffee, satisfied that they had accomplished their mission, I excused myself briefly. I met my deputy outside and told him to not under any circumstances go to that boy's class. What you should do, I said to him, is walk around the science building and return to my office in eight or ten minutes and say that the teacher refused to excuse him. So I returned to my office and shortly after that my deputy returned. Very handsome Benue man, he later died in the Dana plane crash. He came in and said: I'm so sorry, the teacher refused to excuse him. And I said: really, the teacher said that? And Hitler at that point smiled broadly. Good good, he said, you're running a tight ship here Mrs. Laseinde. You see, I knew what was going on. I knew that as a big man he needed me to not contradict him. But also that as a military man he believed in chain of command and was impressed that my teachers were maintaining standards.

Anyway two years later I did have to expel the boy. That's a different story. It caused panic in the state command. But I did what I had to do and the boy was kicked out, though I myself was not in the job for long after that.

WHEN I WAS FIFTEEN my mother died. My father married another woman and I had to leave home. I came to Lagos in 2016. With a JAMB score of 257 I got admission to UNILAG to study accounting. At that time my aunt was helping me with the fees but after two years she couldn't continue and I had to start looking for money. Anything I managed to get was going to my younger brother at home. I made sure he continued to attend school but because of the shortage of funds I myself had to drop out. This is why a school friend introduced me to someone, a man, who said he could get me some work. That man was the one who introduced me to Solace. That is how the situation started. Solace was the first person who took me to the club.

Most of the girls have a guy but I do my thing by myself. I have never stood on the street. Sometimes someone approaches me in the club and buys me vodka and then we see. Sometimes it's a phone call that comes in and I pick up the call and Solace tells me the arrangement. He will let me know whether I should go to Radisson Blu or to Eko Hotel. He has about one hundred girls in his network. You could arrive at the hotel room and there will be four other girls there all to have fun with one man. We have arrangements with senators, governors, ministers and they pay in dollars. Not that that kind of big-man arrangement is so common— there are many of us who are competing for this thing—but if you get it you can make one thousand dollars in one weekend. From that amount I will give Solace three hundred dollars. But normally for the regular situation, the one that I collect twenty thousand naira for, I will give him five thousand.

I am back in school now. I entered another accounting course last year in Cotonou. I have someone who drives me there at the beginning of the week and brings me back for the weekend. In Cotonou I share a flat with two other girls. During the school term I only do this work on weekends. When the term is over I stay in Lagos and do five nights.

It's a money issue. Like now I have seventy thousand naira saved and by Monday morning I must have one hundred and fifty thousand. I just have to find that money. Whether I like the men or not does not matter. What matters is that I have feelings and I now know that they don't understand my feelings. Even my boyfriend last year I had to separate from him. He thought because of my work I don't have feelings so he was having sex with one of my friends. Imagine that kind of thing.

The thing we do doesn't have a name which is why I call it "the situation." The situation is not good for me. If I want to have fun then let me have fun. If it is sex then I should be making love. I am a very religious person but this is not about religion, this is something that comes from myself. Deep down I know I am not supposed to be having sex just because I need money. I'm a human being for crying out loud.

YOUR FATHER NEVER TOLD you? To be fair I don't think either of my daughters knows either. I haven't discussed that period of my life with them. Maybe these things are easier to tell other people's children than one's own. We had a lively group of friends around that time. The core unit was me, your dad, Habeeb Adegboye, and Olu Wonder. Adegboye owned a car dealership and had done very well for himself. Your dad was less active than the others. I think your mother was skeptical of our bad influence. We had all been at St. Gregs together and had stayed in touch. I remember our long nights at Caban Bamboo, Stadium Hotel,

Ambassador Hotel. There was always suya, beer, and music and when I say music I'm talking about Bobby Benson, Victor Olaiya, and KSA. Fela was active too in those years but that was a different social scene. Our scene was juju music and highlife.

The ringleader was Olu Wonder. That man had an appetite for life. He could drink a carton of big Star without blinking. He loved to dance, he loved to laugh. And good for him, he was also the only bachelor among us. The rest of us were married with children and we held responsible jobs. We had people to answer to at home. Olu Wonder was a socialite from a wealthy Lagos family and he was known all over the city. Famous singers like Abiodun sang his praises. Those were the days. Then the days got darker.

Adegboye was from one of the ruling families of Aiyepe. When the Alaiye of Aiyepe died in 1981 it turned out that our friend was the preferred candidate for the throne. As I said he was a man of means and he was seen as someone who could bring the necessary prestige to the role. I'm sure you understand that the people who get picked for these roles come from a pool of candidates who all have legitimate claim but then the person who emerges as the final choice has to somehow be ideal, whether it be in terms of personality, or wisdom, or wealth. From the moment Adegboye's selection became clear we began to call him Kabiyesi, half in jest to begin with but then in all seriousness.

At the time of the investiture ceremonies we all went with him to Aiyepe. It was a series of grand parties, the kind of event no one in our wider circle was going to miss. But the installation of Yoruba kings is not for those who are easily scared. *Àán j'oba* can mean "we are installing the king" or "we are eating the king." The pronunciation is exactly the same so what you hear in it is whatever you want to hear in it. The organization of these things is in the hands of the Ogboni, the cult of elders. Is it true that the late king's heart is eaten? Nobody who is not there knows for sure. What is known is that the rituals of burial and coronation are very sensitive. Adegboye was undergoing a transformation and he belonged to the gods now, he was no longer an ordinary man and he was no longer our friend. On the third night of the investiture there was another party in a series of parties near the palace grounds. What happened that night isn't clear. Was Olu Wonder looking for a bathroom? Was he drunk? He entered the palace, took a wrong turn, and opened a door or two. It seems he caught sight of the new Alaiye who was at that moment engaged in secret rituals with the Ogboni elders.

In any culture in the world there is what can be seen and what cannot be seen. I don't want to single out our culture for condemnation. What happened was deeply unfortunate. The new Alaiye of Aiyepe should not have been seen by ordinary eyes at that moment. That is how Olu Wonder went missing. All his friends were worried. Two days later his body was found in the bush near the palace.

ONE NIGHT THERE WAS a heavy storm and a power-cut at our home in Ilupeju. It was not unusual back then just as it isn't unusual now. We went to sleep in darkness. It must have been in the summer holidays. I was about thirteen. My brother Muyiwa was fifteen and we had a family friend who was with us for a few weeks, Temitope, that's how I know it was summer. Temitope was the same age as my brother. She and her family later migrated to Australia and we lost touch with them. Not long after we went to bed that night the power was restored and the fans came on. I woke up at that point to switch off a bedroom light. I fell back into deep sleep until around 3:00 A.M. when there was a commotion and very suddenly we found ourselves in the middle of the nightmare. The armed robbers were five. Three of them had guns and the other two had machetes. Our immediate assumption was that they killed the gateman to get in. (In fact we never saw the gateman again after that night; our later assumption is that he was in on it.) They rounded us up into the living room and barked contradictory orders, asking us not to make a move but also demanding that we show them where things were hidden. The room was brightly lit. We were on our knees, in our nightclothes, in common humiliation, begging them to spare us. Daddy was shirtless.

It didn't occur to me at the time but in the years since I have decided that they must have been high. Their energy was so intense and their mood was so unstable that I thought there was a good chance they would shoot someone. One of them struck me very hard with the flat edge of his machete. Stop looking at me, he said. He was going to hit me again but one of his mates restrained him and told him to stop wasting time. My face was swollen and a tooth had come loose. None of them had masks or any other kind of disguise. All wore amulets around their necks. We averted our eyes.

They had already brought out the money from the safe. They placed the cash on the table along with a couple of Daddy's watches and the pile of electronics. They went around the house gathering things. Time slowed and my face throbbed with pain. We were huddled in a corner of the living room but they hadn't tied us up. One of the robbers had his rifle pointed at us the whole time. Another drew Temitope to him and said in a stage whisper and with a smile: dirty girl. They ordered Mummy and Temitope into my parents' bedroom and four of them followed and closed the door behind them.

Daddy, kneeling next to me, fought back tears and prayed under his breath. I placed my thoughts elsewhere. Life did not feel real. There was at first loud begging coming from the bedroom and then muffled screams and loud warnings. My brother and father and I tried to keep as still as possible. The clamor from the bedroom subsided. The robber who had been left to guard us was wild-eyed and never removed his finger from the trigger. He couldn't have been more than seventeen or eighteen years old. Ten minutes passed or a half hour and then two of the men emerged from the bedroom and went into the kitchen for beer. They complained that the beer wasn't cold. They sat in the living room and drank. Their attitude was almost bored, as if we weren't there in a corner in fear for our lives. The other two came out of the bedroom a little while later, sweating.

Later when we told the story we always said I had been

struck in the face by the robbers. That was the aspect we told other people about. Home invasions were terribly common in the late '80s. I wonder how many people are walking around traumatized. People would murmur their sympathy and thank God on our behalf that no one had died. Sometimes I was praised for having been brave. As for the other thing, well, even Kehinde only got to know about it after we had been married five or six years.

This past Sunday after church we stopped in Ilupeju to see my parents. On our way back I began to weep. The children were quiet. Feyi is nine now and would probably have guessed that my tears had something to do with his grandma. He might have assumed it was about her dementia. I've noticed him noticing her deterioration over the past three years. Jadesola is only six and less able to guess why I might have been crying. Kehinde simply told her that sometimes even Daddy has very big feelings.

PASTEL COLORS ARE IN: lime green, powder blue, pink, cream. People come looking for a particular cloth, something that is for their matching outfits. They come in, I locate the cloth for them, we bargain, and they are happy. And for me I'm most happy when they discover other things they like and they end up buying more than they planned.

I have been selling lace in Ebute Ero for a long time. I was doing it before I got married. I was with my older sister on Nnamdi Azikiwe Drive three streets away from here. I arrived in Lagos from Abeokuta in 1969. When I began we mostly bought from Indians. They had a factory in Ilupeju.

Then the government didn't want Indians here anymore
and many of them went back to their own country. I'm trying to remember one of their names but I can't. But some of
them used to wrap their heads like this, to cover the forehead. After the Indians were pushed out we ourselves became travelers and we started going to all kinds of places.
The first place we went to was Dubai which is duty-free.
Then we went to China and we went to India. You know
this work we do is contraband. It is illegal to bring in this
cloth. The government says that there are already many
companies making cloth in Nigeria. But you can't fool people: the local quality is not good and the cloth is more expensive. You can't fool a Nigerian woman when it comes to
cloth.

One problem that everybody knows about is that this
country is bad for manufacturing. There is no electricity,
there is no water, there is no security. That is why those foreigners ran away, that is why local quality is poor, and that
is why we had to begin smuggling. Customers come to us
and say they want this or that particular lace. If the high-
quality factories were here why would I worry myself with
all this traveling? But I have no choice. I fly to Shanghai and
go by land to Hangzhou. At the Chinese factories I tell them
which patterns I want and they make them for me. Then we
smuggle the order back to Nigeria little by little through
Lomé or Cotonou. We are patient.

A lot of my business now is being run by Bisola. I always
valued education for her which is why she ended up as your
classmate at that your elite school. But I also taught her that
there is more to life than books and I am proud that she is

such a practical person. She's the one who goes to Mumbai for me now. There's an Indian man there who has been dealing with Nigerians for forty or fifty years. He speaks fluent Yoruba and Bisola knows how to bargain with him. It's a family business for him and it is a family business for her too. They understand each other.

Our culture values cloth. *Eniyan l'aso mi*. If you can afford the Swiss one for fifteen thousand you can buy it here. If you can only afford the Chinese one, as low as two thousand per yard, I also have it. Cloth and society are braided together and cannot be separated. No matter what happens to you in life, no matter how great your happiness or deep your grief, you have to dress for the occasion and that is why people come to me.

WE CANNOT SLEEP WITH both eyes closed. Anything can happen here where the rich are right next to the poor, where even the rich are not so rich otherwise they would not be here. Still some people live in walled compounds and they have quieter generators and their homes are built on solid ground. As our people say, all the fingers of the hand are not the same length. In this city nothing should surprise you. You can never look at a place no matter how wretched and say no one would build a house here. Poor people build anywhere or rent anywhere because they have no choice. In the neighborhood where I live the paved road ends, a dirt track begins, then you come to a downward-sloping path that you can only follow on foot and at the end of that path you find houses clinging to a hillside. Above are the homes of the rich. The walls of their compounds are built right up to the edge of the valley. Below is where we live. No it's not even a valley as I said, it's a gully.

If I could afford better I would live better. I studied agricultural economics and farm management in Ilorin and then I wasted three years looking for a job in the agric sector. Afterwards I came to Lagos and I forgot about all that. I now work as a gateman at Protea Hotel in Ikeja. This cannot go on forever, this is not the life I am destined to live so I am focused on my exit plan. Come back in three years and I will not be here. I know I am not destined to remain in this hell of no roads, no light, no water. I believe I will be in Canada. I am slowly completing the paperwork. God has done it for others and I know he will do it for me. Matter of fact I keep a small flag of Canada in my pocket, not to remind God but to remind myself.

Last month it rained so heavily that the wall surrounding one of the big houses up above the gully collapsed. It didn't happen in the middle of the night, it happened around seven in the evening when people were starting to cook their evening meal. The wall just collapsed outwards and fell into the gully. Concrete and mud, all of it came down. Directly in the path of the collapse was a small one-bedroom house. Two people died that night, a lady and a small boy. I knew them. Mrs. Anyiam and her son of about nine years old. People were just shouting and we tried to rescue them. She died instantly. The boy might have had a chance but there was so much mud. It was dark. He was alive when we finally pulled him out but he stopped breathing not long after.

This is how human life is wasted here. If I did not have

an exit plan I don't know what I would do, maybe I would go mad. Nobody can bring a police case for that collapsed wall, nobody can ask why the engineers built a faulty culvert, nobody can inspect the drainage in those compounds up there. Their runoff erodes the gully with every rainfall and it will always be so. Mr. Anyiam is staying with a neighbor for now. I visited him and his face was like someone had pressed pause on it. Two weeks ago workers began to rebuild the collapsed wall. Everyone who can leave this country leaves. There's a reason you yourself don't live here. In three years I'll be gone. In thirty years Nigeria will be empty.

AFTER WE GRADUATED I got admission to UI to study philosophy. But after one semester there I was able to transfer to law. In those years there were a lot of strikes by ASUU so my course took almost six years. Then I sat for the bar in Lagos and after that went to Jigawa to do NYSC. I haven't really stayed in touch with members of our class, for the reasons you know about. I'm in touch with four or five people at most. Morayo goes to my church. Chinaza and Emman communicate with me on Facebook. After NYSC I ended up not practicing law. My dad has this construction firm and even though I didn't know anything about construction I ended up taking that over after he had a stroke. Well I didn't know anything back then and now I know enough. I know how to delegate, which is the most important thing.

My God you people put me through hell. Everyone says

schoolboys are wicked but I don't know why I had such
particularly bad luck. I wasn't stupid, I wasn't unkind, and I
wasn't so bad-looking as all that. But when schoolboys seize
on something it becomes an obsession for them. I ran into
Damire at ShopRite two years ago. I could tell he was
avoiding me. If you remember he was the main instigator of
this thing. I didn't confront him. I mean, more than twenty-
five years have passed. We greeted each other and left it at
that. But afterwards my mind just kept going back to school.

We must have been in JS3 when Damire decided I
looked like a lizard. It wasn't funny but very quickly others
decided I did look like a lizard. And that was how it was day
after day, month after month. Lizard. I would enter a room
and everyone would start flicking their tongues. Lizard, they
would whisper. You did it too. There weren't any of the
boys who didn't. I tried to counter by calling others by their
nicknames: Big Ears, Squinty, Longthroat, Blackie, all these
meaningless insults we gave each other. But I knew and everyone knew that no one had a nickname as nasty and inju-
rious as Lizard. And I think it was because it was so nasty
that it became the truth. I could see people figuring that if
this person is being persecuted so much he must deserve it
for some secret reason. But there was never a secret reason.
I was just being made to suffer for nothing. I was being
made to suffer because I was being made to suffer. That was
the reason: it was happening because it was happening.

All those years not one single person stood up to say:
OK, enough, let this guy be. Not one person. It just went on
and on, into SS1, into SS2. Years of this stuff, of people nar-
rowing their eyes, nodding their heads slowly in a reptilian

way, pretending to scurry up walls. Damire, as if insisting on his discovery, was always the loudest. My nightmares were brutal at that time and yet they were always so simple. In fact I had just one single recurring nightmare. In the dream I had to put on my uniform and go to school. That was the nightmare. Then I would wake up and have to put on my uniform and go to school.

Things came to a head in our final year. I became silent at home, I lost my appetite, and I started to get failing marks in many of my classes. In the worst twist of all I broke out in rashes as if my own body had turned on me and was taking part in the cruel joke. At one point I thought: why not just kill myself? Why would death be worse than this? My parents could see that something was seriously wrong and my father made me tell him what was going on. The next day he came to school and talked to Mrs. Laseinde. He was so angry. Mrs. Laseinde summoned all four arms of SS3, boarders included, as you well remember, and told you all off. I was so ashamed that my father had to come all the way to GCS simply because I had been given a nickname. This must have been February or March of 1992. And yet between then and June I would still be walking down the hallway and would see someone quickly flick their tongue. I would still see someone mime a scaly hand.

I STUDIED FINANCE IN Lancashire and worked in banking in the oil and gas sector in the U.K. for some years, in Preston first and then in London. Then I came back to Nigeria and did the same thing here through the '90s and early 2000s. I made good money. Now I make even better money in my car importation business. So you could say I've had a normal life, a successful but normal life. But people are curious and they have tried to explain what they see as my one strange habit. There must be something abnormal about the guy, you know. Some spread the story that my wife died young and that this was why I started my annual thing. But my wife is alive, the children are there, I am a perfectly ordinary husband and father. Some others call what I do performance art but to me it's not art and I am not an artist. And of course many say it's morbid. Ignoring death is what I find morbid because death is right here.

The sàárà aspect of it is important because for a man my age when my funeral comes it is going to be a celebration. That is how it is in our culture. I'm not old yet but by any measure I've lived a life. So I rehearse the funeral that way. I envision it as the funeral of someone whose life is worth celebrating. We put up tents, rent chairs and tables, and provide food for the whole neighborhood. All kinds of people come and though the adults are both fascinated and skeptical the children are simply happy to be there. Everyone eats and drinks and while they do so I'm upstairs in the parlor, dressed in a full suit, sealed in my casket for the duration of the sàárà. What I am doing is preparing for the inevitable day. I am not interested in avoiding the inevitable. I don't want to come to that day without having prepared myself for it.

I ordered the casket from New Jersey eight years ago. It is made of bronze burnished a deep brown with copper escutcheons and fittings. It is lined with cotton, satin, and velvet. I find myself really looking forward to the hours I get to spend in there for one day each year. When I'm in the casket I am immersed in a darkness unlike the darkness of night or sleep. This is a very deep, padded darkness and the feeling it brings is one of peace. The casket is set up upstairs and because it has some tiny air vents I can faintly and intermittently hear the sàárà going on downstairs. But for long stretches the darkness is accompanied by a profound silence. Sometimes when I've been in there for a while I hear a low and unfamiliar sound. The sound seems to be coming not from outside but from inside. The first time it happened I was mystified and a little scared. Only later did I realize that what I was hearing was the sound of my own blood circulating through my body, the blood in my own head. I was hearing in a way I hadn't heard before the sound of myself being alive.

IMAGINE YOURSELF OUT IN the city, maybe sitting in traffic and observing everyone around you. What are these people thinking about? This is Lagos so they're probably thinking about money. That is our common condition. Those who have enough want more, those who don't have enough need more. But what else? No one knows about anyone else's inner life. Behind those apparently vacant eyes are problems, plans, and daydreams of all kinds. As for me, on any given day, I'm thinking about music.

We have a long musical history in this country and not only in the so-called popular genres. We have a tradition of sacred and secular music. In church music, my line of work, that lineage goes back to the second half of the nineteenth century. Rev. Robert Coker studied organ in Germany in 1871. So imagine the kinds of places he visited, the kinds of people he met. For all we know he might even have encountered a figure like Johannes Brahms. In the generation after Rev. Coker was Fela Sowande who studied in the U.K. but who was really the first notable person to insist on our own African music as an equal partner in these compositions. Sowande's influence on Nigerian church music was transformative but hardly anyone is aware that he had an influence that extended far beyond Africa. He had an influence even on John Coltrane. We don't know these things. How many of the younger generation know that Herbert Macaulay himself, when he wasn't transforming the political landscape, was an avid violinist? Stepping out of the Lagos heat into his own house in the cool of the evening to play Beethoven sonatas.

I direct the choir here and I am also the assistant organist. In addition I teach music at two private schools, one in Ikeja and the other in Pedro. I studied at CMS Grammar School and then continued my studies at MUSON. I'm very fortunate because my talent was recognized. I had top marks in theory, history, and performance. This is what enabled me to go to Trinity College of Music. But I always knew I would return to Nigeria. This is home no matter how impossible it is and believe me it often feels impossible.

What happened with church music in the past is that it was an elitist pursuit. On the one hand the colonists always wanted to claim that their music was better than ours. That was their mindset and they imposed Victorian musical theater on those among our ancestors that were thought of as a local elite. People were performing Gilbert and Sullivan in Lagos at the beginning of the twentieth century. But the other thing that happened was that the people who returned from slavery—the Brazilians, the Saros, the Cubans—also wanted to keep themselves separate from the indigenous people. But two interventions happened to counteract that. First you had the nationalist movement which candidly asked why we should be ashamed of anything in our culture so long as it didn't contravene Christian principles. Secondly when Sowande and others like Akin Euba and Ayo Bankole integrated Yoruba folk song into their compositions, people were able to see themselves better reflected in the music.

You know, you've found me at my happiest. It is a Tuesday afternoon and I am filling this basilica with my own improvisations. What I was playing when you walked in was based on a theme by Handel. The only audience was myself, at least until you arrived. I get a lot of happiness when the unexpected happens in that way, when I can share my passion with someone who also knows something about this music. Because the other thing this city can do is dull your sensitivity. Maybe because you're visiting it is easier for you to remain sensitive. But for those of us who live here staying sensitive is a daily battle. When I sit at the organ it is an opportunity for my entire body to manifest the music in my head. My spirit expands, my very being expands to fill this entire space and every note I sound out is for the glory of God. There's nothing else like it in the world.

———

I HAD BEEN WORKING with your grandmother for many
years, maybe four or five, when I met Stephen. Your grandmother was a kind lady, not like the people I used to work
for before. We were very close. I even used to plait her hair,
we were that close. She sent me to school and I tried, up to
JS3, but books are not for everybody and eventually I gave
up. Then I met Stephen. He worked as an electrician, he was
a fine boy, with fair skin, the kind of fine boy they always
warn you about. When I got pregnant, before I could even
decide whether or not to tell your grandmother, she said:
"Remi, you're pregnant." She always called me Remi.

Before the baby came I moved in with Stephen into his
mother's house in Bariga. Stephen's mother did not like the
fact that I had been working as a housegirl and she also had
a problem with me being from Benin Republic. She said I
had to join her white garment church. But we are all serving
the same God and I did not see the reason to change from
the Catholicism I grew up with. Anyway the trouble got too
much and I finally told Stephen that we had to find our own
place. That is how we came to live in Akoka and that is
when I started the hairdressing work.

When we were still living in Bariga, Grace had this sickness. We did not know what it was. But for more than a
week she would cry for a long time before falling asleep and
when she was awake she would cry each time she was held
sideways. But if you held her upright she stopped crying. I
was starting to get scared. As a mother your mind can easily

start racing. But one day we decided to go and visit your grandmother and your grandmother examined this child, really took her and looked closely at her whole body and then she smiled and said the child wasn't sick. She asked us to look at Grace's ears. We had pierced the ears and on the left side the stud was pressing into the back of her head behind the ear. It was just the discomfort of that metal stud, that was all it was. This was three weeks before your grandmother was taken to hospital so it was the last time I ever saw her.

The following year I told Stephen I wanted to go home for a visit. He was reluctant to take the time off work and he was also nervous about entering areas he didn't know. But his friend Dapo is from Badagry near the border and he knows French. He would be a good guide at least halfway to my village. So we arranged it: I brought Grace with me and very early in the morning Dapo and I and the baby traveled by BRT bus to Orile Bus Stop and from there we found the smaller bus for Badagry. The journey to Badagry took around four hours. Dapo was very calm and helpful.

At Badagry we met his people—his wife and children—and then we continued our journey, the three of us. At the border we crossed on foot. People in cars had to show passports but those of us crossing on foot just crossed. On the other side of the border we entered an even smaller bus, about the same size as a danfo, which took us towards Cotonou. Dapo asked me if I recognized the landscape but it had been so long, something like twelve years, and my memories were faint. When we reached Cotonou I kept repeating to myself the name of our village: Joko. It was all I remembered. In the bus park in Cotonou, Dapo asked people for the way to Joko but no one had heard of it. Finally someone said, "Do you mean Gbodjoko?" That was when the correct name came back to me. So the person told us to go to Zinvié, that Gbodjoko was near there, and at the mention of Zinvié more of my memory came back and I had to fight back tears.

We hired two motorbike drivers at the bus park. One driver carried Dapo, another driver carried me and Grace. We found the village, a little over an hour from Cotonou. Night was already falling when we got there though there was still some light in the sky. At first no one recognized me. The villagers who came out were wary of us. Then someone said: "Isn't this Renée?" That was when my mother came out screaming. Someone took the baby out of my hands and my mother tried to lift me on her back. She lifted me up and I was on her back. I was already twenty-one years old but my mother carried me as if I was a baby and she was just weeping and weeping.

I WORK UNDER THE bridges. I find a section of concrete that hasn't been taken over by advertising bills and use that for my mural. Of course this being Lagos I have to get clearance. The father of a close friend works at LASAA, the state's signage and advertisement agency, and he arranges the necessary permissions for me. At the moment I'm working at Falomo Roundabout. I only use organic pigments. The white comes from crushed kaolin chalk, the black from charcoal mixed with anunu leaf, the lemon yellow from local river clay, the dark red from ground camwood. I am inspired by the tradition of uli so I sought out people from my mother's family in Anambra who knew the preparation techniques.

For a lot of people in Nigeria an artist is someone who paints on canvas so that rich people have something to decorate their homes with. But if you look back at our native traditions most of our practices could be called public art. Our dances, our masking, our festivals are presented to a public audience. You have to be there in the community to witness the event. My attitude to my art is similar. I'm not too concerned about money or the usual artistic accolades. Even though I occasionally get invited by foreign institutions I don't rely on that. For me it's about how I can weave myself into the texture of the community's life. In other words I want to live up to my responsibility.

When I have selected a bridge I talk to some of the area boys under it. I let them know I'm an artist and that I'm going to spend a few days there. I usually give them a small fee the same way I would if I were parking my car somewhere that was under their control. I give them at most a thousand naira per day to share among themselves no matter how many of them there are. I find the one who presents himself as the leader and deal only with him. Once I've settled them they serve as a buffer between me and any further aggression in the space. They start calling me Aunty Adaeze, the "aunty" being a mark of respect. The work fascinates them and some of the best conversations I've had about ecology and habitat loss have been with these "uneducated" men. I ask them to tell me about their home villages and what kinds of interactions they had with the natural world growing up. Immediately their eyes light up. They become like boys again.

For the drawings I focus on animals in the Nigerian habitat that are critically endangered. I've recently done two dragonflies, for instance, from a subspecies of damselfly called flatwing. I've done a toad called Perret's toad which is found in only one place in the world: around the Idanre Hills in Ondo State. Perret's toad adapted itself ideally to this beautiful ancient landscape and now it is on the verge of vanishing forever. In fact it hadn't been seen since 1970 until a team of scientists located a small population in Idanre in 2014. All other common African toads lay their eggs in water but Perret's toads spawn semiterrestrially sometimes laying their eggs on vertical rock faces. The uniqueness of each animal is what moves me. The survival of such an animal is good for its own sake and it is valuable for environmental biodiversity. But it also has symbolic value. What I mean is that the natural world is always telling us stories. The days I spent drawing two large Perret's toads under the bridge at Ikeja Bus Stop focused my mind very powerfully on the potential loss of this creature, this creature of such resilience that its tadpoles can hatch on a vertical rock face.

The one I'm doing at Falomo now is about the Niger Delta red colobus monkey. Because of hunting and deforestation there are probably fewer than five hundred of them left in the wild from a population that used to be over a hundred thousand. The Niger Delta red colobus (I love how simultaneously musical and awkward the names of animals can be) is one of the most endangered primates in the world.

Why should such a magnificent creature be on the verge of no longer existing? As I apply white clay and red camwood dye to depict the monkey's fur, as I paint the monkey into being stroke by stroke, I feel I am engaging in a kind of public mourning, as though I were soothing the body of the dying animal. And while it is true that most Lagosians have other things on their minds than species loss we are also a very spiritually alert people. It's not hard to initiate conversations with our people about the decline of ancestral knowledge. We used to know how to relate to the earth and our myths are full of lore about the lives of animals. I find Nigerians very sympathetic to this kind of thing and I think it is what accounts for the dreaminess in the attitude of the boys under the bridge when I ask them about their memories of their villages.

My work has vulnerability built into it. The animals are disappearing out there in nature and the work itself mirrors that disappearance. The drawings don't last very long. They remain on the walls for a few weeks at most and after some time has passed all that is left is a ghostly trace, often just in the parts of the drawing on which I used charcoal. Sometimes I spend three whole days drawing, making this very meticulous work, and by the fourth day someone has rubbed it off or has covered it with ads. But I accept that too. It doesn't matter how the image is erased, whether by rain or by human hands, whether by nature or by culture. What matters is that I was there, that I spent those hours, that *it* was there, that it existed and flourished for however long it did.

WHEN THE STATE GOVERNMENT decided to improve some of the roads in Amu Ewa the decision was not only to tar the roads but also to widen them. It was not a matter of demolishing people's houses, all they were going to do was alter the houses that were encroaching on the expansion path. The government offered the owners money as compensation for slicing through protruding parts of their homes. All along Ita Oba you could see these half houses neatly cut with their interiors facing the street. Whether or not the owners accepted the money the houses were cut. As you went along the road you could see the colors of different rooms visible to the outside world, a patchwork of pink, green, blue, and white rectangles demarcated by the gray borders of concrete walls.

The Methodist cemetery in Amu Ewa is along Ita Oba. The outer edge of the cemetery overlapped with the new road plan and as it happened Dad's grave was one of those affected. The families, ours included, were informed and told that the government would pay for the exhumation and relocation of bodies. We consented to it as we didn't really have a choice. Back when we buried Dad the day was overcast but the day we exhumed him years later was bright and hot. It was a small group at the exhumation: me, your dad, and the three laborers. Mom didn't want to be there. I can't imagine what must have been going through your dad's mind having buried his twin brother and then being there twenty-six years later to exhume him.

When the laborers had dug down they discovered that the casket had disintegrated. That wasn't unexpected. What they didn't anticipate was the body's state of preservation. We were all taken aback. Dad looked like he had been in there no more than four days. There was mud on him and his skin was whitish but he looked like himself, like a younger version of your dad. It was a real shock and we were all trying to figure it out. Later on I thought that perhaps there were substances in the ground that had helped preserve the body. Maybe the chalky nature of the soil had something to do with it or maybe there was toxic runoff from the cement production facility on the outskirts of town. But none of that explained why the other bodies were not preserved, why it was only Dad. The cemetery laborers were really spooked. Word got out and what people said was that Dad had been a person of such saintly character that his body had to remain uncorrupted. I was just a kid when he died and nearly my whole life I've been hearing everyone say what a good person he was. But to see him emerge that day shifted my thinking. It was as if his early death had been a metaphysical error. It was as if his body was refusing the fate that befell him, as if this whole time he had been awaiting a fairer judgment.

I AM TWENTY-SEVEN AND my thing is tits. I am crazy about them. Someone once said it had something to do with not having had enough motherly love. I don't think that's true. What's true is that I want a girl whose tits are enough to rest my head on. The other day I was in a situation with two girls and one other guy. We were at the guy's house playing truth or dare. "I dare you to suck her nipple," that kind of thing. The wilder of the girls said to the guy, "I dare you to put your dick in her mouth." The other girl had a Christian vibe and didn't want any part of all that. But the guy unzipped and shoved his dick in her mouth. She was shocked, she started shouting, she said she was going to sue. Sue? Where does she think she is? We were laughing. She left, very upset. But I think she must have settled down later.

Anyway after she left I dared the wild girl to give the other guy a blowjob. And once she started blowing him what was I going to do? I'm not into spectator sports. So we had a threesome. Then the guy called some other girl he knew and we were four again and that was super too, symmetrical. Orgies happen at every level in Lagos. This is not about rich or middle-class people. I'm not rich. Everyone is religious but the body is not firewood. I like to say that in Nigeria we are theoretical Christians and practical Satanists.

But you have to be alert about who you get involved with. There are girls my age who drive Range Rovers. I know one, a schoolteacher, who also has her own place in Lekki. It doesn't take a genius to figure out what's going on when a schoolteacher is driving a Range. Every girl on every level does this kind of thing. Show me one person who's not compromised, I'll wait. What you have to watch out for though is locking. Most especially if you're fucking a girl who's not at your level. Do you know what locking is? She might be looking to capture you. She gets a sample of your semen, takes it to a babalawo and that's it, you're locked. It happened to me. I fucked this Ijebu girl and ever since that time I haven't been able to perform with Lucia. For more than a year now I haven't been able to get an erection with Lucia or with any other girl. I thought to myself, is this just a guilty conscience? That would be funny because I haven't had a conscience in a long time. Is it nicotine, is it alcohol? But no, I really do think the Ijebu girl put a curse on me. No offense but you Ijebu people have a reputation for having some of the strongest juju in all of Africa. There was this woman some weeks ago, my neighbor. She's a sex maniac, I think. Definitely a sex maniac, in my professional opinion. Old, probably in her late thirties already, but sexy as hell, really incredible tits. You look at them and all you can think of is pillows. Anyway when I was on the phone with her telling her everything I was going to do to her, I was hard. But when I showed up at her place and got naked I found I couldn't get it up. I was so embarrassed.

I fuck without protection. Not because I don't believe in AIDS—I saw a lot of that in medical school, it's a terrible disease—but because I don't think it's that contagious these days. I somehow don't think it can catch me. Make no mistake though: I know there's evil in this world. Some of these girls are dangerous enough to use "jazz" on you. And I think there's something a bit sad about really knowing that there's evil in the world, like, really knowing it and then having the ability to just carry on like it's nothing. That's sad. What I'm saying is that my situation is sad. Have you seen *The Dark Knight*? I read somewhere that it really messed Heath Ledger up. There's something good about that, it means there was still some innocence in the guy. It got me thinking about how nothing can mess with *my* head anymore. I just carry on. Two guys and two girls, three guys and one girl, four girls and one guy. There was a time when even the notion of an orgy would have shocked me. I was such a sweet little kid. My innocence is gone.

I was in secondary school the first time I wanked. Like most people I discovered it by accident. My hand went wandering and just started doing its own thing. But I remember how when the stuff surged up my entire body was like: wow, this is wonderful, this is *beautiful*. That's the day I really became myself. Then in UNILAG full sex began and I haven't stopped since then.

IN 1997 I RETIRED from teaching theater arts in Ibadan but my family is from Lagos and I was raised in Isale Eko. We are Awori people. After twenty-one years at the university in Ibadan it made sense for me to come back. I have this friend, Mrs. Ademulegun, who is the kind of person who's always looking for opportunities. I prefer not to think too much about those things but she's one of those business-minded women who's always after the next chance. Anyway shortly after I retired (an early retirement, I was only fifty-two at the time) I was casting about for how to occupy my time. That was when she told me about this property in Surulere.

The house and land belonged to a widow whose late partner was an Italian. The lady still had a bank loan against the house and she wanted to be done with it. I told Mrs. Ademulegun there was no way I could afford anything that expensive and that I didn't know why she had even suggested it to me. But at the same time I ran into this banker I used to know, one Mr. Chibuike, very decent fellow. Chibuike said he could arrange a bank loan for me with UBA, which is where he was. He got me seven million naira and in combination with my severance pay from the university that put me in a situation where I could buy the widow out and begin to redevelop the property.

I knew I wanted to build a school. Schools were booming businesses at the time. A private school was springing up on every street and it was the kind of thing everyone thought they could do. But my thought was that I could do something more specialized. Since my sister is hearing-impaired and I have always been sensitive to needs in that area I thought I would open a private school for the deaf. I already knew British Sign Language. I undertook some additional training, I did the research and began to make plans. It wasn't meant to be an NGO but I also knew it wasn't going to be a money-spinner. I poured all my severance pay which was around three hundred thousand naira, significant money at that time, into the project. When the school opened we taught at the Junior Secondary and Senior Secondary levels. Private school standards vary widely in Nigeria and there's little government oversight. People just do whatever they want, really. Or where there are rules people circumvent them with bribes. But I don't like being an unserious person: if you're going to do something do it the right way.

The school made a real contribution. Some of my graduates are people who feel they wouldn't have had a chance to function in society; the education they had at the school made all the difference to them. Remember we are talking about a society where people still think deafness is contagious, we are talking about a society where deafness is considered the same as mental retardation. Just yesterday one of my former students, a girl named Bright, came by to see me. She was so energetic and joyous and she reminded me of the school plays we put on. We once did *Macbeth*. I mean there's something about *Macbeth* that always works well in an African context, all those witches, all that blood and struggle for power. It's like reading the metro section of the *Punch* or the *Sun*. But there was the added layer of staging it in a hearing-impaired context. I always say there's ability in disability and when you see youngsters like Bright signing Shakespeare it transforms you. "Out, out, brief candle, life's but a walking shadow."

Unfortunately the school just wasn't viable after a while. It was hard to find teachers who knew British Sign Language. And even though our fees weren't very high and we offered scholarships we still found it difficult to collect payments. The whole operation was hemorrhaging money. Eventually I was propping it up with my own pension and that couldn't continue indefinitely. So I said let's wind this thing down and start something else. And that's how I redeveloped the place as a night spot and got some young men to run the place. At least it's paying for itself now. People say: but Mrs. Iyinola, a night spot isn't like you at all. And I always tell them: a person can be many things. Business is business and money doesn't smell.

MY HUSBAND IS PARTICULAR about his shirts. Either he washes them himself or he takes them to the cleaners. Not long after she came to live with us Charity washed one of them without his permission. Predictably it wasn't clean enough for his standards. He complained about the collar and the cuffs and asked her not to touch his shirts again. But she went behind his back and the second time around did a perfect job. What choice did he then have? He surrendered and she now always cleans his shirts. I tell you this to give you a sense of the kind of person she is. She is incredibly self-motivated. The reality is that some of these girls are luckier than others. Someone who ends up with me and Chibuzor will be treated in a humane way. But many others find themselves in bad situations. At her former place Charity was raped by the husband and of course she couldn't tell the wife. She couldn't tell anyone because no one would believe her. In fact she told me only because I questioned her the day I hired her. I asked her about her background, where she worked before, why she left, and so on. She's a pretty girl though she dresses too provocatively sometimes. But the thing is that Charity had helped raise four of this man's children. He and his wife were planning to send her to school. Then the rape happened.

Anyway months after I hired her I was out one day and I sent my driver Baba Sunday home to drop some things off. He went inside the house and attempted to force himself on Charity. When I got home that evening she told me what had happened. I didn't want to bring it up with the driver but

Chibuzor said I should. So the following day I asked him and
of course he denied it. But earlier that day I had overheard
Charity talking to him. Normally they don't talk. So I asked
her what he was saying and she said he was asking whether
she refused to greet him because of what happened yesterday. That's one sign she was telling the truth. The other is
that the cook told me that Charity said that I didn't believe
her. So I said: Charity it's not that I didn't believe you. I believe you. I just want to give everybody a fair hearing.

I could have fired Baba Sunday but what's the point?
He's an old man, over sixty, a Christian, an elder at his
church. None of that is an excuse but I don't think he will
try it again. I did say to him: I want you to know that I
know you did it. I know that the girl isn't lying. It was a bad
thing to do, it was bad. I confronted him and just left it at
that. I just make sure now not to leave him alone with my
own children.

I live in a building with four flats. One of my neighbors
recently hired a girl and after a while I noticed that the girl
was sullen. So I called the girl aside and said: the woman
who hired you is very nice. If you're not comfortable here
you won't be happy. You have to make yourself comfortable. The girl then confided in me that when they took her
away from the last place they told her she was going home.
But they tricked her and put her into new employment.
That happens a lot and these girls are kind of lost. To make
matters worse they usually don't have phones or any means
of communicating with their people back at home. The
whole housegirl system is brutal in that way. Another of my
neighbors keeps her housegirl locked outside the house dur-

ing the day while she herself is out working at the airport. Why would someone do that? The housegirl is made to sit in the hot sun in front of the house all day long from morning till night. Because my neighbor is afraid the housegirl will steal something. Can you imagine? Why would a human being be so wicked? But it's not just housegirls. People abuse their girlfriends. Wives get beaten. These things happen more than you might think.

I ONLY USED TO smoke cigarettes. Not long after I started the job with Mr. Korede, Lawrence came to work with us. When I told Lawrence that I had problems eating, that I often didn't feel like eating, he introduced me to marijuana and said it would make me hungry. And it's true I started to eat more but then I got addicted to marijuana. I used to go over to the Hausa guys near the Long Bridge, the ones who sell rams. They have shelters there where people smoke all kinds of things. Marijuana turned me into somebody I'm not. My character changed. Things that I would normally handle carefully I began to handle them anyhow. Even the day I walked away from my job I had smoked. Later I realized that my character was no longer recognizable to me, that this thing had altered me. So I started crying to God that he would make a way, that he would let that evil spirit leave me.

The day I quit I had also drunk vodka. I was out of my mind. Days after I realized with regret that I loved having this peaceful job. I don't want to do any job that's going to hurt me. That's why I want to come back here. Maybe you can beg Mr. Korede for me. He didn't hurt me, he gave me everything, I am the one who misbehaved. I already talked to him and he said they have employed someone else and there's no more work. But maybe if you beg him for me he can forgive me and take me back. I have changed my life. I am born again now actually. For seven days I was sleeping in Best Living Church. I was praying and fasting and I believe the evil spirit came out of me. Then I left the church building but I had no house to go to. For the past three days I have been sleeping in an uncompleted building in Isheri. Everything I own is in a small bag that I keep in a tailor's shop. All my money is gone. When I had the job I used all of it to buy drinks for my friends. Now there is no money left. If I don't find help soon I am afraid this city will finish me.

I am just going down and down. I have thought of returning to Agbor but I just cannot go back there because I cannot face my mother with this shame. And I cannot go back to Warri. There are too many bad gangs and they will take me on the wrong path again. My main problem now is I have no money. I am just going down and down. I have not eaten since yesterday and the hunger is dealing with me. Even when I see food I don't want it anymore. As you are looking at me now you are looking at somebody who is falling. The evil spirit has come out but I am falling.

THE PEOPLE WHO CALL in are not calling to talk to me. What do they really know of me? They are calling to be heard and to hear a sympathetic voice on the other end of the line.

That voice just happens to be mine. There aren't many places in this city where such conversations can actually take place, where people don't feel judged for their level of education, their social class, or their command of English. And of course it is radio so appearance doesn't come into it at all. The callers don't have to make themselves presentable and mostly they have no idea what I look like. All they know of me is my voice.

And what is that voice? Many things at once: young enough that they can call me by my first name, mature enough that they can confide their heartaches to me, seductive enough that they feel included in the game of intimacy, innocent enough to stay within broadcasting rules, feminine enough that it fits men's idea of a beautiful woman, strong enough that women can sense that I am no pushover. And then there are their own voices. Four nights a week I find myself inside this forest of accents and I absolutely love it. There are numerous varieties of Lagos accent from the posh to the unvarnished and there are accents inflected with the residue of various native languages and there are also British and American accents from people who have never even left Nigeria.

Whether the conversation is about love, money, or family all the complexities are heightened by the fact of this being Lagos. People love to talk. People want to tell you about being stuck in traffic, they want to tell you about the time they got swindled, they want to vent about how bad the service is in restaurants, and they certainly want to tell you about matters of the heart. Every week it seems there's some version of: I thought we were together but I found out

she's been dating another man. Or: even after we had a
baby together he won't leave his wife. It's rough out there.
What can I say but "eeya." The word contains multitudes.

I listen and I dole out equal parts sympathetic affirma-
tion, encouraging laughter, and sensible advice. It works because I know I am having a simultaneously light and serious
interaction with a person whose life I know very little about,
a person whose beliefs are probably quite different from
mine. I steer them away from politics not because politics is
dangerous but because it is boring and boredom is one thing
we can't risk on radio. At the other extreme given that these
are strangers and we are broadcasting live my producer and
I are always ready to end a conversation before it spins out
of control. But cutting the conversation off because someone is being aggressive is rarely necessary. People actually
know how to behave.

Hosting has made me respect my fellow Lagosians.
Every single person you see out there on the streets, every
face in every crowd, is someone who has had to solve difficult problems today. It sounds a bit sentimental but it's true:
this city tests one's patience daily, it's a daily exam, and I
make a good-faith effort to imagine what people are going
through. This is something I picked up from yoga. When
we are talking on Fresh FM in this very public setting something personal is being transmitted. You can sense the
human being over there on the other end of the line. I don't
solve anyone's problems, I'm not a doctor or therapist or
priest, but I think people are consoled by the mere fact of
being able to call a stranger in the night or of being able to
overhear others doing so. My show is a space for softness in

a city that doesn't have too much of it. No I should say that
a different way: there's a lot of unheard softness in this city
and my show is one of the places where that softness can be
heard. It's three or four minutes at a time of something that
we categorize as entertainment but that actually contains
something far richer.

It's so strange to me that I ended up doing this work. I
studied architecture. I was going to be the good daughter
and join my dad's firm. But life had other plans. It turned
out my voice was my biggest talent which is funny because
in school I was teased for how deep and brassy it was. As
for my being in a long-term relationship with a woman, not
everyone needs to know about that. Some people know,
most don't. What counts is that I remember where my center is, where my grounding is. Love is the center. Everything else flows out of that.

THAT NIGHT I LEFT Costain Roundabout around 5:30 and
immediately entered traffic. It had rained earlier and the
roads were flooded all the way to Ojuelegba and on to Ji-
bowu and beyond. Tola had texted me to say I should avoid
the expressway because a fuel tanker had overturned at Ore-
gun. Such tanker accidents often lead to terrible fires caused
by people trying to siphon off the diesel or petrol. My best
bet was Ikorodu Road, she said. It was slow going. People
were wading in the streets and I could only imagine what
things would be like in Victoria Island at that moment. V.I.
is a perennial flood zone but the government is building a
new city on landfill in front of it, a filled-in section of the

Atlantic, for sure the worst idea I've ever heard, a monu-
ment to a future disaster. As I went across the mainland I
kept thinking of all the encroaching water and its eventual
and inevitable vengeance. I spent an hour and a half on
Ikorodu Road going slowly past the orthopedic hospital in
Igbobi where my aunt had been a surgeon, slowly going
past the once serene neighborhood of Palmgrove where I
had lived as a boy and where I could now see the black
plumes of smoke from unidentified small fires and then past
Obanikoro where my dad had taught at the Baptist Academy and past Maryland where I had done my first three
years of primary school. A shifting array of people selling
goods moved between the cars. I had not noticed before
how every stretch of this route contains personal memories,
how the city is like one of those movies shot in a single take
from the window of a moving car. By the time I turned onto
Mobolaji Bank Anthony Way the sky was dark and the air a
mixture of exhaust, spray, and mist. Traffic loosened a little
bit at Leventis but became congested again near Lagos
Country Club. Here there was flooding too and the Keke
Marwas went by with their wheels half submerged. It was
nearly 8:00 P.M. The night was alive with the noises of car
horns and street vendors. At Ikeja Bus Stop under the
bridge I saw what looked like two enormous frogs drawn in
chalk almost floating above the surface of the concrete and
strobe-lit by the headlamps of passing vehicles. As I made
my way through the confusion of cars and danfo buses I saw
the used-clothing merchants of Ikeja and their fluorescent-
lit stalls. Squeezed between two of the stalls a man crouched
to defecate. On passing the dueling statues of Fela and Awo

on Obafemi Awolowo Way I was reminded of the night I
had encountered the lunatic policeman who had tried to
strangle me near the Allen Avenue junction and how I was
saved only by Tola's legal training and quick thinking. It
was now 8:30 and I was inching past the Ikeja City Mall
when I heard a great boom and saw a large fireball rise into
the sky about half a kilometer away in Alausa. Curiosity got
the better of me and I drove into the neighborhood where a
panicked crowd had quickly gathered to witness the sudden
pandemonium and add to it. A tanker had caught fire and a
nearby bank was in flames. Thankfully the building and the
tanker were both empty because of the hour or so the dis-
traught gateman claimed. People were running haphazardly
shin-deep in water, helpless to do anything about the conflagration, their sweating faces glowing in the flames. After
half an hour I came out of the Alausa detour and entered
traffic again and set my car homeward on that night when
the city was drowning and burning at the same time.

SEVEN

WHEN HE RETURNED TO THE CITY HE REALIZED THAT IT IS crisscrossed by water to such a degree that a more accurate description would be that it is a body of water crisscrossed by stretches of land. The city is oriented on an east-west axis with a lagoon above the axis, an ocean below it, and numerous inlets, creeks, and canals in between. But this factual description simply vanishes once it is asserted that the city actually has a north-south orientation with the city flaring out on either side of a long thin river, the tributaries of which radiate outwards the closer it flows to its delta. When the citizens are asked whether their city runs from east to west or from north to south they seize on one and only one of those descriptions and do not entertain the other as anything but superstition. For those for whom the city is hemmed between lagoon and ocean the city has always existed and is of stable size and population. For those for whom it is oriented in a north-south direction the city was a village barely worth the name until the nineteenth century, a village that experienced explosive growth in the twentieth century and keeps on growing in the twenty-first century, farther and farther north, hardly getting wider but each day flourishing upward like a sapling into the heart of the continent. The north-southers emboldened by new wealth say that it was precisely this disagreement with the east-westers that led to the internecine war of the late nineteenth century during which multitudes who shared a language and lineage slaughtered each other and at the end of which the ruling family of the city changed for good. The east-westers betraying only the faintest trace of bitterness sit in their living rooms which are full of ornate inherited furniture and say there was never any such war. When you examine any of the maps in those east-west homes you find that there are only two cardinal points represented, east and west. For them north and south do not exist and anything beyond the bounds of the lagoon is a fiction.

But when he returned to the city he saw that it could best be compared to one of those computer terminals at an investment bank the face of which is always a cascade of figures conveying arcane information about the deals, trades, anxieties, and changes of the financial system, not only because an unusually large number of people in the city are indeed involved in the so-called financial services industry where sums of money are moved around according to algorithms to produce nothing but misery for human beings but also because all the inhabitants of the city regardless of their actual jobs are obsessed with the mystical properties of numbers. In their newspapers and radio shows and in the hubbub of voices that can be heard in the streets the talk is of fractions and percentages, of interest rates and profit margins. Nowhere else has he seen such long lines outside betting shops as men and women await their turns to place wagers on distant events like horse races and boxing matches. In lieu of a national religion there is the lottery which confirms in them the brutal intuition that life only makes sense when there are a few winners and numerous losers. Those among them who know calculus are honored as princes and those with a grasp of statistics are venerated as priests. Speculation is rife, hysteria barely contained, and the citizens bet on anything including whether inflation will rise from 15 percent to 20 percent, whether the price of bread will double in the coming year, and which of two ripe oranges will fall first from a tree. The economic situation is perilous and the people take refuge in playing games with numbers in a futile effort at vengeance for the way numbers play games with them.

But when he returned to the city he found that one cannot escape the feeling of moving through a stage set. The shadows are too crisp, the vistas too neat, the houses, one would think, are made of cardboard, the banks of plywood, the schools of Styrofoam, the bridges mere projections or backdrops as in a painter's studio. But in contrast to the flimsy environment of the city the people have an unusual solidity. Each person in this great and vast city is fully embodied as though each were a film star in an alternate reality. If the city itself is two-dimensional its denizens are four-dimensional. They have beautiful skin darkened by the sun and they walk elegantly not out of any calculation but because of the easy pride they take in their own limbs. And though they range from the very thin to the very fat, each of them is so at home in their body and its abilities that they all seem to be exactly the right size. And more than walking elegantly they are concerned with dancing well which for them has nothing to do with tutored steps and everything to do with an instinct for the groove. It is true that they are not without a certain arrogance for they say of foreigners who can't dance that such people are "making the dance weep." For these citizens being in the body is key and they do not despise in themselves the tendency to ignore the intellectual aspects of life in favor of the corporeal. Seduction is in their ethos a great and worthy pursuit so they seduce each other all day long, their bodies smelling of sweat, pheromones, and the restlessness of life. It is a city in which people make love with the tremulous joy of first-timers, the solemnity of undertakers, the insouciance of professionals, the vigor of perverts, and the untiring ardor of immortals in whose every movement is a promise that there will be more where that came from tomorrow and the day after that. Confronted with this sybaritic paradise the traveler might wish never to leave but soon exhaustion creeps in and with it the suspicion that pleasure is not always pleasant, that indeed there might be something rotten beneath the glow and that the only thing to do with this realization is to travel on.

But he returned and saw how the city glimmered on the horizon like a silver thread, a mirage one keeps approaching without ever reaching until all of a sudden one is in its center. The city has no outskirts: either you are still a long way off or you are suddenly surrounded by the crowd. The crowd is all that exists here and the meaning of existence in this city is to be with millions of others. The rulers grasp at their petty privileges but the streets are democratic. Things flow and function without government help. Besides, what would the people do if they had to surrender their favorite pastime of complaining about politics, that great abstraction before which they can deposit all their heartache? The city is unique in having neither aristocrats nor untouchables. Its citizens are radically equal. This is not to say there aren't superficial differences of appearance but no one is in doubt as to how temporary and contingent those appearances are. The billionaire today could be in prison for fraud tomorrow and the beggar contorting himself for pity in traffic this afternoon could by this time next year be the possessor of limitless wealth. No condition is permanent. The point, they insist, is not just the changeability of circumstances but memory's vulnerability to oblivion. Every day is new in the city. That is why there are no antiquities just as there is no technological innovation and that is why the citizens live in the ever-evolving present. It is a city in which seconds, hours, days, eras, seasons, notions of earliness and lateness all exist but in which there is no word for "time," as though time itself, separated from practical purpose, were a theoretical construct for which they have no use. In this city of crowds the citizens sometimes come out en masse into the largest squares and broadest avenues to demonstrate the raw fact of a population. They seem to believe that when they bring their bodies together in public all things are possible.

But when he returned to the city he found himself contradicted at every turn. Many houses in the city are built with adobe and other such humble materials but roofed with a shiny metal of extraordinary versatility and durability. The malls are pristine with a porcelain gleam but the shops within them sell only rough handmade goods. The organization of the streetscape is such a hodgepodge that at times he thinks he is looking at installation art but the appearance of haphazardness quickly gives way to the realization that everything set before his eyes is carefully chosen and that a delicate balance has been achieved between apparent opposites. Swift decision-making is characteristic of the people of the city where in two seconds and with a single haughty glance the women can determine the true price of a bolt of cloth and declare it either cheap or covetable. Throughout the city this talent for accurate and rapid distinctions between flavors, colors, scents, building materials, auto parts, and musical instruments is rampant and extends even to the caskets in which they bury their dead. This is not an ability they deploy simply to entertain or impress one another. The citizens are not shallow connoisseurs. Their x-ray vision is rather a matter of survival in a place in which chance plays such a large role and in which fate always threatens to darken the skies and deluge the day. For those whose sense of accuracy is not well honed the city can be as trackless as a forest and as hostile as a hall of mirrors. One wrong move could be fatal and so no one makes a wrong move. It is the reason a stranger should never set out into the city without a native guide. Some cities have a plan, a diagram of the city before its founding, or a map, a schematic representation of the city as it now is. Not this city. The choreography that keeps it going would be amazing could it be seen in a single encompassing moment. That is not possible in a city which changes faster than it can be described and which tolerates cartography only on a scale of 1:1.

But on returning to the city he found it grim and was tempted to call it a post-traumatic landscape except that would have suggested the trauma was in the past. It is a city of unspoken sufferings: the wordlessness of the disappeared dissidents, the blankness at the other end of the blackmailer's phone line, the hush after a lynching, the shiver after a beating, the abyss following child abuse, the stillness after a murder, the muteness after a rape, the long-held hopes that vanish as soundlessly as a drop of water on velvet. This silent devastation is one face of the city, the face you see if you arrive in the city during the day. But should you happen to arrive at night you might think you were in a different place altogether. From over there is a sound of argument, from over there a clamor of complaint, from over there a gospel choir, from over there the muezzin's call, from over there three or four sputtering generators, from over there the squall of the bus stop and taxi stand, from over there revelers and water sellers, from over there the neighbor's relentless television blaring out soap operas, from over there disconsolate wailing, from over there passionate lovemaking, from over there disputation and rancor, a vast sonic mix of an ocean that beats its incessant waves the whole night through until sunrise arrives and the pale light of morning settles a dazzled silence once again over the city.

On his return he thought he was thinking of a photograph but he realized that he was thinking of a photographic negative, the colors inverted and left and right flipped. But it became clear to him that what he was actually thinking of was a photographic negative that had been made but had gone missing before it could be printed. And finally he realized that no, the negative had not even ever existed, it was all in the imagination or it was all in the future and he was thinking of a picture that existed only in the mind of the one who was thinking it. The more he tried to describe it the more elusive it was. It was there but it could not be looked at directly. At best it could only be seen out of the corner of the mind's eye and this was the way one might begin to speak of the city. Since ancestral time the people of the city like all people who have inhabited the earth have been curious about what the future might hold for them and how they might get help for the variety of ordinary problems faced by human beings, the problems of marriage, children, sickness, employment, as well as the daily difficulties of modulating one's feelings of fear, anger, lust, and jealousy. The citizens sought out the oracle who spoke through the divinatory abilities of priests skilled at interpreting the codes and combinations of natural phenomena. That oracle remains till this day and its language is as subtle and confusing as ever and as incontrovertible. And yet for each problem there are better and worse solutions, so the people continue to search through the gods, through money, through poetry, through the movies, through the reading of leaves and clouds and constellations for ever-better paths out of the problems of being human. The path is spoken in the mysterious language of four, sixteen, sixty-four, two hundred fifty-six. He is moved by the time he spends among the people in that city of mysteries because they truly are a humble people and they know that the city always knows more than they do. Like reeds they bend with the wind in order not to be broken by it. They pursue wisdom instead of mere knowledge and wisdom is always there in small manifestations, always imperfectly seen like a long-desired photograph coming into visibility from the bottom of a developing tray, the gradual appearance of a face that is none other than their own.

But he returned to that drowning city, that burning city, which is the ruin in the present of an empire that will never exist in the future. In this city of permanent ruin improvement is not possible and so the inhabitants have no dreams of improvement. Rather every night in their deep collective sleep they dream of a perfect city which in their dream language is a house that cannot be fixed but only knocked down and rebuilt and in that way perfected. These are not daydreams, they are real dreams and the dreamtime is busy with the activity of construction. The dream-citizens meet nightly and rebuild the razed city with elegant parks, sustainable infrastructure, humane architecture, and inclusive principles. They build from perfectly rational blueprints, bringing the city to perfection each night. They work all night on the dream city and in the morning they wake up exhausted without knowing why. They trudge through their dispiriting days in the real and prematurely ruined city which has no hope of being improved. When night falls they return to their dreams and do it all again, building the ideal and evanescent city for the umpteenth time. These citizens are unaware of the commonality of their dreams and if they were to be made aware of that nightly joint labor they might have a chance to direct their efforts towards the real city which they have essentially abandoned. But the paradox, he realized, was that they couldn't be merely told. They have to know it, it has to somehow well up in their spirits, the truth that there is no such thing as an unimprovable city and that their energies are better expended on the real. If they are merely told but don't know it in their hearts and if this knowledge does not come to all of them at once it would be of no use.

But when he returned to the city he noticed that for once nothing at all had changed. You enter the city by crossing a sturdy suspension bridge into one of those wide and impressive modern highways until the city looms up before you with its low houses, its riverfront, its malls and car dealerships and beyond them the high-rises and skyscrapers of the central business district. The roads are covered in all the expected contemporary advertisements and the people without engaging in any extremes go about their daily lives, each absorbed in his or her or their concerns, the nurse, the kindergarten teacher, the policewoman, the carpenter, the sex worker, the clergyman, the petty thief. All judgment aside no city could be more normal or ordinary than this one. No city could give a firmer and less obtrusive illustration of the idea that all cities are essentially the same wherever they might be located on the world's map. But slowly at first then rather intensely he noticed that something wasn't quite normal about the city after all. He crossed another suspension bridge and came onto the modern highway, a different one but very similar to the one he arrived on before. The high-rises and skyscrapers and malls and car dealerships were there and yet they were new to his eyes. It was not a matter of amnesia: they were genuinely different, similar to the other set but just different enough to be noted as such. He felt his awareness transformed when he saw a nurse walk by, a different nurse from the nurse he saw earlier but also startlingly alike. And then he saw another kindergarten teacher and another policewoman and another carpenter and another sex worker and another clergyman and another petty thief, all looking almost exactly like the ones who went by before. Walking carefully through traffic was an old man with trembling hands carrying a tall but light sculpture wrapped in diaphanous white fabric. Five minutes later he saw the man's twin brother carrying the sculpture's twin sculpture. This is a city of doubles, a pluripotential city of echoing selves and settings, as though it were a poem each line of which wishes to be read twice. The game then was to make sure not to miss any double. He saw each shop twice, he got two glasses of wine instead of one and the singularly beautiful man who smiled at him from across the broad table at the municipal library turned out not to be so singular after all for later on at the second library there was a second singularly beautiful man with the same enigmatic smile. This world that has its spares everywhere is an enjoyable world because it offers a form of immortality. Even when there's loss the substitute is there awaiting use and for that reason the citizens move around without fear, in freedom and felicity and anyone who visits them begins to enjoy that freedom as well. He thought he might want to stay in this city in which the age-old conundrum of scarcity had been solved, that he might want to live in it forever. But one day coming down a second street in a second neighborhood for the second time that day he saw himself walking towards himself, his own self or a twin he never knew he had. The twin's face was his, the twin's gait was his, the twin began to speak and when he spoke the voice was a perfect copy of his. This harsh confrontation with the possibility of his own replaceability was too much to bear and that very evening before darkness had fallen he left the city.

EIGHT

———

THE LARGE NUMBER OF YOUNG FAMILIES HERE NECESSITATES preschools. During my working day I sometimes see a line of toddlers trooping along the sidewalk in front of my studio. A teacher at the head of the line, another at the rear. The children are organized in pairs. They hold on to a plastic walking rope and sing "The Wheels on the Bus." When I look out I see the segmented brightly colored crocodile making its way along the sidewalk.

I am at the studio early to print out photographs from my trip. Printing the photographs is like truly seeing them for the first time. I will have seen each image on the digital display of my camera at the time of making the photograph. I see it again on the computer screen when I upload it. If the image is one I want to show Hana or send to Stefan then I also see it on my phone. But these immaterial views leave the question of the size of the photograph open. The photograph has no size until it is printed; the size is not something I can know in advance. The pixel dimensions are not the true size of the photograph, only a code for its possibilities. After I print the photograph, usually at 5"x7", I then know whether it needs to be larger or whether it needs to remain small or even whether it doesn't work at all as a photograph. I might discover that the colors fail or that the composition fails. I stick some of the printed photographs onto the magnetic board in the studio or I tape them to the wall or I glue them into maquettes.

The digital folder of ongoing work is named "Search Party." Of the hundreds of photographs I made in Lagos in December only twenty-two are set aside for further consideration. These are not the best of the images. They are the ones that tell me in one way or another that they might be part of a sequence with other images. In the folder now is the material I've been gathering since the publication of *Tree of Heaven*. The slowness of the accretion itself guarantees nothing. Most of these photographs will fail.

The photographs from Lagos are tranquil, suggestive of human presence, charged with human absence. They are portraits of unpeopled scenarios, planks, tires, culverts, basins, stones, ships, plants. I fear the demands that portraits of people make. Portraits are high risk and require familiarity, vulnerability, and strangeness. I have also developed an aversion to the theft of anyone's face. For portraiture not to be a theft I would have to be even more patient and intent than I am now. In any case what do faces tell us about the truth of places? And yet, to emerge from the clamor of Lagos with such unpeopled stillness feels paradoxical.

FROM A FAMOUS QUESTIONNAIRE: *when and where were you happiest?* The way it is phrased makes it seem as if the questioner is asking for a retrospective view from the end of a life. It seems to assume that the happiest moment has already happened. When were you happiest? To answer *I can't know yet* could be accurate but it wouldn't respect the spirit of the question. The spirit of the question is: *what has been your hap-*

piest moment so far? Maybe it is easier to imagine future moments of some happiness than it is to imagine that the happiest
moment of all is yet to come. We often feel the happiest moment is in the past. The happiest moment was fleeting and
intense and not deemed happiest at the time. It was only
thought so later because of how the passage of time has burnished it.

DURING MY TRIP TOMI and Kehinde often made Nestor available to me as a driver. He was from Akwa Ibom though he
had grown up in Lagos. In his constant smiling was an un-
trustworthiness. One day I asked him to take me to Ikeja
GRA where my family had lived for a period in the '80s.
Many of the houses in that neighborhood are large white vil-
las set on extensive grounds. We had never been rich but
Dad's work as a state commissioner had brought us a fleeting
moment of privilege the most visible aspect of which was a
house with a pool that we did not use and a shady lawn at the
back in which the twins and I played ball. Back then we had
a housegirl, a gateman, and a gardener and once a month a
man came to tap fresh palm wine from the palm trees behind
the house. From time to time my parents strung up lights and
hosted cocktail parties on the grounds.

The house was on a quiet side street. Nestor parked on the
main road and I walked towards the street. The neighborhood had changed. The street was now blocked off with a
security gate. A pair of armed men at the gate eyed me but let
me through. My interest was less in the house than in the
surface of the street leading up to it. When I was twelve I was
walking to the video rental shop to return some tapes when a

dog had suddenly appeared. I was afraid of dogs back then and took off at a sprint. The dog gave chase. The chase must have lasted only fifteen or twenty seconds but those seconds were a pure and never-forgotten terror. Eventually I tripped and went flying onto the tarred surface of the road. The moment I fell the dog stopped and trotted away. I was badly bruised with most of the damage on my forearm, a long laceration from the right wrist almost all the way to the elbow as though the arm had been unzipped. On the walk home I came close to fainting from the pain and gore. When I arrived at the house my sisters screamed. I needed stitches. The dark keloid scar remains.

I knelt down to touch the road and the gatemen took a tenser interest in my presence now but remained silent. In the years since the incident I had made my peace with dogs. I understood better the role my irrational fear had played, understood better the sensitivity and intelligence of dogs, their need not to be feared. Later in the car I asked Nestor where all the stray dogs in Lagos were. There are very few around now, he said. He looked in the mirror and tried to assess the tenor of my question. People catch them, sir, he said. They catch and eat them and some people call it a delicacy.

My surprise was feigned. I had only wished to hear it from him. I had heard the same thing already from Tomi, that most of the strays in the city were gone and that even pets were at risk. Tomi had told a story about how in the compound where he used to live a neighbor's six Alsatians had gone missing one by one. And there had been a story in the newspaper about an articulated vehicle transporting dogs from the north getting into an accident. Many dogs had died in the crash and

the newspaper headline had said "Scramble for Meat as Vehicle with 500 Dogs Crashes." The crash had happened near
Calabar in Cross River State. The reporting had a whiff of
stereotype and invention about it: in the too-neat number of
dogs, in the typically Calabar names of Bassey and Edet (an
alleged survivor and a doctor respectively), in the lack of
photographs from the scene, in the absence of follow-up stories. I asked Nestor if he himself had ever eaten dog meat. He
smiled. His eyes darted in the rearview mirror but he said
nothing.

IT IS MIDAFTERNOON. SADAKO is asleep when I get into bed. I
don't know how to take naps but she can always take one
when she needs to. I place my hand on her back. I can feel
under my fingers the ravine and the two long hills to either
side of it. My fingers settle along that landscape. In deep sleep
she breathes quietly. I turn my hand so that now it is the back
of the hand that rests in the valley of the small of her back.

INGMAR BERGMAN'S *WINTER LIGHT* takes place over the
course of a single day in rural Sweden beginning with a
church service in one underpopulated parish and ending with
a church service in another. It is a film about the fading away
of faith, demonstrated by the sparsely attended services that
bookend the film and also by the personal struggles of the
parishioners and their pastor, inner struggles that make up
the bulk of the film's action. Interiority is hard to show but
Bergman is good at it. A wife and husband come to the pastor
after the first church service. The man is a fisherman and he
seems reluctant to speak about his troubles. His wife talks

more easily. It is she who has dragged him in for counsel and she tells the priest what has been happening. Here in rural Sweden, far away from it all, or so one would think, her husband is troubled by global problems. Specifically he is terrified by what he's been hearing on the news and seeing in the papers about Chinese people: that they are raised to hate, that it's only a matter of time before they acquire an atom bomb. The poor man's face is blanched by the horror of this unspeakable prospect. The pastor responds by acknowledging the helplessness we all feel and he advises the fisherman to trust God. In saying these words the pastor is trying to help the fisherman manage his anxieties but the pastor finds himself unable to believe what he himself is saying. To make matters worse he is in the throes of a bad flu and doesn't feel very much like himself. All this adds up to the fisherman not believing him either. Life goes on, the pastor says wearily. Why must we go on living, the fisherman shoots back.

The fisherman's wife is the soul of hope, one of those people burdened with a talent for seeing the bright side of things. She thinks maybe it would help if the two men were able to speak privately. The men would rather be spared such an ordeal but she insists and her husband takes her home and comes back to the church alone. The pastor asks him about his life: his physical health, his financial situation, his relationship with his wife. All of that is fine, the fisherman says. So it's just this Chinese thing, the pastor says. They are at an impasse. The fisherman's despair only encourages the pastor to speak in candid and confused terms about his own doubts. He confesses to a lack of faith in God. And if the world is so cruel and there is no God, the pastor says, why go on living?

These words discomfit the fisherman. The one who was to help him has slid into a morass of his own. What had been a look of horror on the fisherman's face now becomes a look of embarrassment. Too full of his own troubles to help his spiraling pastor, he leaves. Word comes to the pastor later that afternoon that the fisherman has shot himself in the head.

WHEN I SAW THE toddlers go past a few weeks ago I was convinced for a moment that I was seeing prisoners being transferred from one holding unit to another. The next time I see them the thought returns and it feels slightly less surprising: these are prisoners, they are being transferred. Then it happens again and now each time the toddlers trundle past what was a somewhat random thought has become an inescapable one. I am unable even to say for sure if the little ones are holding on to the walking rope of their own free will. No they have all been bound to it, latched to each other, compelled into a forced march to the unending tune of "The Wheels on the Bus."

THE CLIP HAS NO voice-over and only depicts a roaring crowd on the streets. It has the feeling of a raw file but it isn't one, it has been edited. Later on I see other footage, from Tehran, and that footage with its larger and more passionate crowd is more widely circulated. But I am fascinated by the initial footage from Kerman, by the humble crowd and their chanting and singing, by the black and brown and dark blue of their somber clothing, by their responses to the unseen calls of a man with a megaphone, and by the mysterious spectacle of two large monochrome flags in red and black held aloft above the crowd. Also held aloft by the hands of unseen people is a large portrait of the dead man.

The assassination of Qassem Soleimani in the first week of the new year darkens the world with the possibility of war. He had close-cropped hair, a white beard, dark eyebrows, and a glowering manner and he was the most esteemed and most feared member of Iran's military. Following his assassination there are immediate threats of vengeance from Iran followed by counter-threats of escalation from the United States. But amid all this, the rites of death. The funeral also takes place in Kerman, his hometown, four days after he is killed and it is a massive event, full of angry men, some of whom weep tears of pathos and fury. There is a stampede at the funeral and dozens of mourners die, death added onto death. The following day a Ukrainian plane crashes a few minutes after takeoff from the Tehran airport. The hundred seventy-six people on board are citizens of many different nations and all of them perish. That is how the year begins.

WALKING AT NIGHT IS a consolation unless you're worried about violence. Otherwise the night is a lightly woven blanket which covers and soothes. The source of its beauty is the same as the source of its danger: everything that exists in daytime exists at night but is now seen with a shallow depth-of-field or with a dimmer. Months pass before I return to the hedge on Kirkland Street. It is a photographic problem I haven't managed to solve yet but I think now that what I need is a nighttime shot of it. At the back of my mind is the possibility that the private-property man might see me and that he might be even more hostile because it is night. In front of the hedge I latch the camera onto the tripod and set it to a fifteen-second exposure at ISO 400. I'm about to begin focusing when I get a strong feeling of uneasiness. I don't examine the feeling. I don't second-guess myself. I simply step back and without even detaching the camera fold the tripod and walk away.

COMING OFF BROADWAY AND turning onto Quincy you find the Harvard Art Museums (plural name, single large building) which has been extensively renovated. The renovation is out of sight and the façade has been kept traditional and quiet. There had been a collection of smaller museums that had specialized in different areas, the best known of which was the Fogg, then the museums were merged. Near the front entrance of the building as it now stands is an oval blue plaque placed by the Cambridge Historical Commission in honor of Louis and Elizabeth Agassiz whose house once stood on the site. Inside the museum one immediately forgets the modesty of its redbrick façade. A colonnaded courtyard soars upwards, getting lighter and airier with each successive floor, the pale plaster of the original interior gradually replaced by glass and steel. The modern materials above are carefully interposed in the same proportions as the columns at ground level, retaining the classicizing feeling of the old building without direct use of classical ornament. Above the fifth story the entire space is covered by a transparent atrium of glass that affords a vertical flood of daylight.

Entering the elevator I see Emily and I feel joyful at my friend's face. She is with two people and we can't talk much but she tells me she's been to Chile since we last met, to work with the large telescope in the Atacama. She doesn't expect to be teaching this term, she says, but she'll send me a note soon. I ascend on the elevator and enter a small gallery on the third floor in which are several limestone reliefs from fourth and fifth century BCE Persepolis, each about thirty inches high. Three depict, full length and in profile, servants wearing loose-fitting clothing and soft cloth caps, one servant on each plaque. Two of the reliefs are in a more sinuous style and one, from a century earlier, is in a crisper and more severe style. They might have been part of a frieze placed on a palace stairway to evoke a procession. The context was either dining or sacrificial. On one plaque a servant carries a lamb. On another a servant holds a bowl in each hand. In the third (and earliest) a servant with one foot raised on a step before him cradles a bowl with his left hand and holds its matching hemispherical lid in place with his right. It is this final gesture, so delicate and familiar, that I find most memorable, this moment of gentle touch preserved in present tense for two thousand five hundred years. I think not only of the meaning of the servant's action but also of the skilled sculptor whose adze and chisel shaped every swell and dip of his hands and of the meticulously carved bowls. I think of the skill it took to carve the belts and caps and the faces in profile. I think too of what can no longer be seen: the limestone chips gathering at the ancient sculptor's feet, the faded work of the painter who covered these now monochromatic surfaces in malachite, cinnabar, and azurite.

I hadn't planned on making my way to this particular room and maybe my being there is purely coincidental. But I can also sense that I'm acting reflexively. The drums of war are beating in a distant place and we begin to think about art and culture, we begin to connect what we enjoy to what is being destroyed or what is at risk of being destroyed. We respond to geopolitics with a kind of automated humanism, with consoling but suspect appeals to "our shared humanity." I remember how my neighbors dragged me out to dine at an Afghan restaurant in October 2001 on the weekend the American invasion began, I remember the uniquely American stupidity of dining out on Afghan food on a night when Afghans were being incinerated by our government.

This is the first time I'm paying close attention to the Persepolis reliefs. Opposite the display case are four photographs that I am surprised to see among the coins, seals, and sculptures of a much earlier era. Three of the photos are from Iran, the fourth is from Azerbaijan, and all were taken by Gilles Peress in late 1979. They correspond geographically with the ancient works on display in the room. ("Taken" I say when describing other people's photographs but for mine I default to "made"—because I can vouch for my own intentions?) Peress's calligraphic photographs show an expert ability to balance forms across the picture plane as though he has taken the rythmic perfection of Cartier-Bresson to the next level of complexity. I recognize a couple of the photos from his influential photobook *Telex Iran*. What isn't clear is if the curators only recently brought these photographs into the gallery to draw attention to the suddenly newsworthy matter of Iran.

In teaching my students to examine texts and think about

history I tell them to always stay alert for the "uh-oh" moment, to be primed for that incident in which some additional wickedness emerges in the conventional story being told. The Persepolis limestones entered the university's collection as the bequest of an alumnus, Grenville L. Winthrop, a rich lawyer and famous art collector whose property at his death in 1943 was inventoried at more than four thousand objects, among them Maya and Aztec sculptures, European and American paintings, Egyptian bronzes, and Chinese jades. The Winthrop family had been powerful for centuries and their power had been accompanied by acquisition. Grenville Winthrop was a direct descendant of the first governor of the Massachusetts Bay Colony, John Winthrop, and owed much of his wealth and eminence to this lineage. Two years after the Great Colonial Hurricane hit southeastern New England in 1635 with a force never since then equaled, John Winthrop's troops massacred hundreds of Pequot people at Mystic Fort. Following this genocidal war Governor Winthrop retained as part of his spoils a Pequot man and two women and enslaved them in his household. Some three hundred years later his descendant Grenville Winthrop purchased the Persepolis limestones from the Brummer Gallery in New York. Brummer Gallery had bought them from the dealer Azizollahoff in London in 1936. How Azizollahoff acquired them is not known since by 1932 the Iranian government had banned the dismantling of Persepolis by European archaeologists. The exportation of artifacts from the site was forbidden. Gently the servant begins to lift the lid of the serving bowl. A disreputable provenance is nothing out of the ordinary in these elegant, light-filled, climate-controlled rooms.

AT DAY'S END IN the week between Christmas and the New Year in Lagos I went to find the place Nestor had told me about. The roads and bridges were unsteady in the smog. Inside the Hausa market I picked my way along a path between rickety buildings so shadowed in its narrowness it was as though night had fallen already. The sand-filled sacks with which the path had been firmed as protection against the annual floods made for an uneven gradient. At that time of day there were few customers at the market. The listless shopkeepers sat in front of their stalls. One wooden structure, larger than the other stalls, was covered wall-to-wall with red rugs. Like the shopkeepers the custodian of this makeshift mosque sat in a meditative state in front of his structure.

A minute farther in where the maze of shadowed paths was now more open to the sky almost no shopkeepers were to be seen. And just a little farther the market came to an end. The final structures were two wide sheds beyond which was the muddy river. One of the sheds was empty and derelict and from the other came the tinny sounds of fuji music from a radio. A large pot was cooking some kind of meaty pepper soup. There were young men in groups of three and four seated on benches in air thick with cigarette and marijuana smoke. A table was set up to sell joints, cigarettes, and non-alcoholic drinks. I sat down, greeted my neighbors on the bench, and ordered a Coke. The seller asked if I wanted a smoke and I shook my head. He asked if I wanted pepper soup and I said no. I didn't ask him what was in it. The crowd was eleven or twelve men in all and conversation among them was sparse. From time to time one of the men would get up and dance in a self-forgetful way, twitching and trembling. The others did not watch these lone dancers. Each man simply focused on his bowl of pepper soup or smoked his blunt or cigarette and stared into space. Their bodies spoke of work: lean frames, muscular limbs, set jaws, resolute faces that now were slowly relaxing into day's end. These men were physical laborers, bus touts, abattoir assistants, cattle herders. Near the riverbank was a small dog playing with her three pied puppies. A man came in wearing the white uniform of the National Union of Road Transport Workers complete with yellow epaulets. He greeted some friends, lit up a joint, and began to dance.

When I finished my drink I stood by the riverbank. The river was so choked with garbage that it was on its way to becoming a landfill. Some distance upstream, on a rise, the lights of houses shone in the dusk-dimmed air and were reflected in the water. Over there the water was cleaner. A few yards from my feet the puppies on the bank played with their mother. They were beautiful dogs, basenjis, the kind that don't bark. I stepped back into the shed and only then noticed a fourth puppy, a tiny one hardly bigger than the size of a hand. It was playing by itself under the seller's table, tumbling in the smoke-filled den.

EMILY EMAILS TO ASK me to call. I call. She sounds tired. She's been talking to our student Anouk about her undergraduate thesis. What Anouk has submitted so far is brilliant, Emily says. She has advised her to go down to the Wolbach Library at the Harvard College Observatory and look into the material they have there on the work of Henrietta Leavitt. I say I haven't heard of this scientist and Emily tells me more. Leavitt, who died in 1921, worked at the observatory for thirty years. She hadn't been able or rather she hadn't been permitted to design her own studies at the observatory or even to operate telescopes. Such opportunities were simply not granted to women at that time. But she had attended Oberlin and Radcliffe and had shown a keen talent for astrophysics. Her work at the observatory was to painstakingly inventory the stars recorded on the university's photographic glass plate collection. By comparing plates of the night sky photographed at different times and carefully annotating the thousands of stars for relative size and brightness she was able to make a major contribution to the ability of astronomers to calculate the distance of Cepheid stars. Her annotations are still there at the observatory, Emily says, meticulously written in her hand and she was but one of hundreds of women who worked as human "computers" for the observatory. Looking into who they were and what they did would be a great boost to Anouk's study.

There's a seriousness in Emily's voice and I can tell Anouk's undergraduate thesis isn't the main thing on her mind. Then she comes to the matter: colon cancer. It was discovered at the beginning of December. She has been in treatment since then. Nothing can prepare you for this extreme of tiredness, Emily says. I am fighting it, of course.

There's always a chance. But the chemo is doing such a number on me that I sometimes want to be done with it, with the chemo, with life, all of it.

Silence on the line. The silence goes on so long I think we've been disconnected. And then she goes on. I come to my senses, she says, and all I can think about is how to grasp these months, weeks, whatever it is I have left. These months, these months. I think: God, let them be months rather than weeks.

IN ONE OF HIS speeches Soleimani described Trump as a gambler. He also said that his fellow Iranians know how to be martyrs. In reports by American news media in the aftermath of Soleimani's death these comments are omitted but another part of the same pugnacious speech is cited. We are where you do not expect us, Soleimani had declared. But it was he who had been taken by surprise, it was he who was found and killed, an irony the American news outlets enjoy.

The world is tense. On social media are those who cheer for war. Reading these experts and those who only believe themselves to be experts I can see the blitheness of their tone, their detachment from the real consequences of war and the casual cruelty their detachment allows for. When these people declare that the important thing now is war with Iran they say it not at all caring how many people are already suffering in Iran or how many people are likely to suffer in the case of a war. What they seem to care about is not having to change their essential faith in American superiority, a superiority which can only imagine other people as disposable terms in the search for power and wealth. The political solipsism is harder to bear with every passing year. It is ever more painful to witness the cruelty towards distant others that passes for international politics in this country. What they think of as foreign is not foreign to me. Foreign is my people, every city looks to me like Lagos, any act of violence towards such places is easy to imagine as violence towards people I love. To see devastation visited on some defiant and doomed population out there is to imagine that same devastation falling on the people I think of as mine.

I am watching a French TV series. A French spy hopes a Syrian woman he loves, who has been arrested and tortured under the misapprehension that she too is a spy, will be freed by the Syrian government. The French spy is a double agent—he is giving French secrets to the CIA—so he tries to use his access to the Americans to get his lover freed. The plot is complicated: he has to give the Americans something they want so that they can give the Syrians something the Syrians want so that the Syrians can free his lover. What the Americans want from the spy is his help recruiting a high-placed Iranian who has access to nuclear secrets in Iran. The French spy tells them he can do this. What the Syrian government wants is for the Americans to bomb a town recently captured by Syrian rebels. The spy agrees to recruit the Iranian asset in exchange for which the Americans agree to bomb the town in exchange for which the Syrian government agrees to free the French spy's lover.

That it is a fictional series does not temper my disgust. How lightly the idea of the bombing of a town is treated, how easily the destruction of thousands of lives can be equated to one man's longing to save one woman. Told in its simplest form it is a story about one white man in Paris arranging for a personal reason to have thousands of Arabs whom he does not know killed. It is emphasized in the show that the town is under the control of anti-government rebels not the Islamic State. In other words even by skewed Western standards this is a blameless and ideologically neutral population. And yet the decision to obliterate them is presented as one person's slightly distasteful quandary rather than as a monumental crime.

The problem is that the series is well made. It is well acted, thoughtfully paced, and meticulously produced. It would be less irksome if it were not so watchable. As I watch I become distractingly aware of how my sympathies are always being directed towards Paris and never towards Raqqa, Damascus, Tehran, or Algiers. Most of the characters, regardless of origin, are depicted as having both flaws and admirable qualities and the direction is subtle by the standards of most television. This is what I find increasingly grotesque: that something objectionable has been so carefully designed to be received as unobjectionable or even as admirably candid. I am being directed to keep looking into the handsome face of the French spy, to continue to care about the unfolding narrative of which he is the center, the close calls, the brave decisions, the plot twists, to let all of that matter to me even though the essentially sympathetic protagonist is someone who is willing to glibly send thousands of people to their deaths (within the series this incident is a very small plot point). The entire narrative frame coerces me into viewing him as "complex" and "troubled" rather than monstrous, rather than an agent of inhumane horror.

But it's good to have a sense of proportion here, I tell myself. It's only television. And anyway, how different finally is this character from so many others? He is only one of the many heroic or heroized white characters who commit crimes that are not figured as crimes because the crimes are committed against foreign nobodies. But no, no, I have to stop making excuses for what I find upsetting. I have to respect the part of myself that is upset by what is upsetting. Halfway through the second of five seasons I stop watching.

SHE IS LYING DOWN on the narrow sofa reading a book. The sofa hardly has room for two. I lie down next to her a bit lower down, a head's length lower. She sets her book down. I rest my head between her neck and shoulder. Slowly I adjust my head until it rests in the hollow between her neck and shoulder like a smooth stone resting in the hollow of a hand.

MY FATHER WAS FIVE when my grandmother died. He barely remembers her and the faintness of his memory has translated all through his life into an intense bereftness at having lost her so young. He reveres the anniversary of her death and he brought us up to do the same. My other grandparents died much later, each of the three of them in a different decade. The twins and I remember none of those later anniversaries because we were not taught to. But we remember the death anniversary of our father's mother who died well before our own mother was born. In December I went to Amu Ewa to visit the grave sites of all four grandparents. My father's mother died in childbirth before the age of thirty. Her gravestone bears no birth date and the child from that pregnancy, my father's sibling of unrecorded gender, did not survive.

It is now the seventieth anniversary of her passing. I call my father and there isn't much to say to him but I know it's important to him to have the moment marked. Later in the day it's the lineage from the other grandmother that the twins and I discuss in our chat. Taiwo has new details unknown to us, lore about our grandmother's ancestor that one of the aunts has recently relayed. The ancestor Esude, the black-smith, that last holdout before Islam swept through the family tree, had a peculiarity we didn't know about: apparently he never smiled. The story that Aunty Wura told Taiwo was that when Esude was young he had insulted the wife of a younger blacksmith. Such was that man's shame that he resolved to commit suicide. It is a big thing in Yoruba tradition to have someone kill himself on your account, *kí enì kan kú sí e l'órùn* (to have someone die on your neck). This man had confronted Esude and in his presence slit his own throat and Esude was marked for life by that trauma. What Esude had witnessed meant for him the loss of any possibility of mirth. He vowed never to smile again. He never smiled again. The story disturbs and fascinates me deeply. Passing by a mirror later in the day I look at my face and search it for evidence of this unsmiling ancestor.

WINTER LIGHT. A MAN in Brooklyn was drawn to the idea of service to the earth and he left a legal career in order to throw himself into manual labor at a composting facility. As his experience in his new role increased one of his main tasks was to organize the large number of volunteers who were also drawn to that composting work. He showed them how to collect and sort food scraps, how to clean and store the wheelbarrows and buckets, how to recognize piles of matter in various states of decomposition, how to use pitchforks and shovels to aerate the pyramids, how to feel with each task a sympathy for the organic processes from which modern life has estranged most of us. He carried out this work for a decade. Before that he had been an activist lawyer for gay rights, taking on high-profile cases. But his vision had evolved to become both more capacious and more focused. He wanted to know what constituted care of the earth at a time when so many others were careless of it. He could see that some were working to rescue the future but that most were undoing that work through inaction. The man was married and he had a daughter, friends, and admirers. His commitments were intense. He immolated himself in the early hours of a Saturday morning in a Brooklyn park.

MY LATE FRIEND'S SON Lucas is a sweet-natured and introverted man with a nervous laugh. He doesn't look like his father unless one looks closely. The father was short, the son is tall. The father was built like a boxer, the son is slim and unathletic. But who's whose father and who's whose son doesn't really matter. Together we are drawing an absent shape. The son is a stranger to me and friendship is nontransferable. Even as we sit down to lunch I know I will do my duty and move on. I needn't become friends with him. He has a husband and two children. He has fine hands and an unsteady gait. The husband is white. We want whatever it is that can help us draw the absent shape, we look for more information, more data points, an ever-greater accumulation of stories and remembrances. But the quest is never finished, the one who went away never returns. Slowly the bank of stories is depleted. The memories evaporate.

THERE'LL BE TIME IN life enough for grief but in Bamako last year I dared believe I was happy, not only at seeing the music live but also at experiencing it in its native habitat among people who knew the meaning of the words being sung. When the singers came offstage they were still speaking languages that were not exotic to the great city around them. After two extraordinary nights I was prepared to be disappointed on the third. It was a Sunday and there was a more substantial crowd at the Chameleon even at our early arrival. Naïny was with me as were Laurie and Paul and some other photographers and filmmakers who had heard about the place from us. The band hadn't taken the stage yet. There was a DJ playing Nigerian pop, Burna Boy's "On the Low," and people were swaying at their tables. A couple was already on the dance floor. The DJ's set went on for about half an hour before a solo guitarist came onstage. The guitarist was turbaned and he sang in Fula in a high plaintive voice and played his guitar in the feedback-heavy desert blues style of Tinariwen. His set was brief, no more than twenty minutes, but it was spacious and majestic. Then he made way for the night's main band, Les Diplomates, the name of whom was a clear homage to the great dance bands of the post-independence period. One of those bands, Les Ambassadeurs Internationaux, had started out as Les Ambassadeurs du Motel de Bamako until politics forced them to leave Mali in the early '70s. They had regrouped under the new name in Abidjan. They had numerous successful international tours and President Sékou Touré of Guinea, patron of the arts and later pitiless despot, was a major champion. To Touré was dedicated "Mandjou," an epic praise song that to this day remains a guilty pleasure for anyone who both digs its groove and thinks about its meaning. Sweetness and darkness: it was the era of the West African super groups, among them the rival Orchestre Rail-Band de Bamako from whom Les Ambassadeurs had poached Salif Keita, and the Guinean flagship ensemble Bembeya Jazz National. In that age of optimism when the colonial shackles were newly off and the future was bright, state-sponsored ensembles presented a cosmopolitan mix of Caribbean, European, American, and African music, a musical modernity with an unmistakable local inflection. Some of the bands included in their repertoire the traditional songs of various ethnic groups but the kora, balafon, and traditional drums were supplemented with modern instruments and sometimes supplanted by them. Whatever was played was played with focus and with that effortless virtuosity that is a byword for Manding musicianship—but one should never call virtuosity effortless.

The performance by Les Diplomates that night began with a song I couldn't identify but which through its rocking back-and-forth rising and falling figure I could instantly relate to others that were already in my musical memory. There were two singers, a man and a woman, both under fifty, the man's tenor light and strong, the woman a raspy contralto. As is so common in the vocal music of this tradition the skillfully phrased songs often veered close to being spoken. There were moments of acceleration when many words were packed in at the end of a musical phrase and dispatched with a flourish, deployed sculpturally, shaped to fill the air as each singer wished. The rhetorical texture of this kind of song, in particular of the call-and-response sections, reminded listeners of the origin of this material in praise song or epic. But this was pop music, not ethnography, and its essence eluded full description. Behind that night's fine vocalists was a cadre of instrumentalists: two guitars, bass, saxophone, trumpet, and drums. The lead guitarist who was an older man had been a member of Bembeya Jazz in his youth. To say someone is doing something effortlessly is to betray ignorance of the effort they put into it.

One song led to another. Swaying became dancing. The dance floor filled up. The low red lights helped as did the company of friends each of whom was getting individually lost in order to be collectively found. The night called out to other nights of desire and satiation like the cold night we danced in Harlem or that time on Victoria Island when the vice president's daughter had too much to drink or that night in São Paulo when we went to Avenida Liberdade or that other night of Amapiano among strangers in Cape Town, that night in Beirut, that night in Berlin, that night in Bogotá.

Something exists in spite of everything else we know to be true of the world. Life is hopeless but it is not serious. We have to have danced while we could and, later, to have danced again in the telling. The lead guitarist of Les Diplomates picked out the opening notes of the classic tune "Beni Barale" and a great shout went up from the crowd. There were ecstatic dancers all around me. The music became a wall of sound and, instructed by the groove, my body moved better than I knew.

THE STUDIO IS CALM this morning. Hana and I work quietly on sequencing for an exhibition. As we work we are listening to *Blue World* the 1964 recording by the John Coltrane Quartet that was rescued from the vaults and commercially released last year. When I listen to Coltrane and when I think of listening to him I remember one of the central glimmering facts of his life: that both his grandfathers were preachers in the AME Zion Church. The keening so evident in his playing sounds like an outflow of that heritage received from two black men preaching the Word of God in North Carolina in the first quarter of the twentieth century. Coltrane enfolded into his sheets of sound the eloquence of the AME Zion Church but also the wilder and weirder dissonances of Holiness practices. His choices are musically driven but in his spirit is a consistent preference for ecstasy over entertainment. Every note he plays is air from his body, every song on these albums a transcript of his breath.

IN THE LATE SUMMER of 2012 a little more than forty-three years after he became the first human being to set foot on the moon Neil Armstrong died of heart complications in Ohio, the same state in which he was born. That same day the *Voyager 1* spacecraft passed the heliopause and entered interstellar space, the first human object to have done so. On board *Voyager 1* which even now continues its journey into the far reaches of space is the Golden Record, a gold-plated copper disc phonograph of various sounds from earth. The sounds include music, rainfall, animal cries, and voices of greeting in fifty-five languages, none of which is Yoruba.

LUCAS SPEAKS MORE FREELY than I anticipate. He tells me an unexpected story and I know he's telling it to me precisely because we don't know each other. I recognize this wish to reveal intimate secrets to a stranger, a wish that contains the unspoken understanding that we will have little contact with each other afterwards. The story is a parting gift not the beginning of a closeness.

He married young. His husband who works for a development agency was on assignment in Port-au-Prince in 2010 and had been there for almost a week when the great earthquake struck. He flew back to Houston and arrived shaken having escaped with his life but having seen horrors. Their older child was only six months old at the time. The husband's serious and sober relief at being back home soon gave way to a depression which he found his way through with Lucas's help. Witnessing so much destruction and human pain hadn't been easy, the husband had said. In the space of a few seconds multitudes had been buried alive under concrete. Lucas had been supportive. Years passed and life regained some sort of balance. I listen sympathetically as Lucas speaks. I mention Sadako's experience of the Great Kobe earthquake and my own experience of 9/11. I say something about how when we come close to the terrors of nonexistence we feel confused about why we are the ones who escaped.

He nods a bit impatiently and comes to the nub of his story. Last year his husband, for reasons still not clear, told him the story behind the story of that week in Port-au-Prince nine years earlier. There had been a boy. "I should say young man," Lucas says, "but boy is what my husband said and that seems right to me." His husband had met the boy before on a previous trip and this was a reunion. The boy was careful and so was Lucas's husband. They weren't carrying on openly. The boy had a job in town working on logistics for foreign organizations, that was how they'd met. But because Lucas's husband was known to be married and because the boy was from a good family—they were not wealthy people but they had a strong moral code—the affair had to be clandestine. His parents, his brothers: it would have been disastrous to be found out. (Lucas didn't elaborate about the brothers but I immediately envisioned macho thugs.)

Lucas's husband had access to a colleague's car. He suggested a lunchtime picnic in the hills outside the city. It was a Tuesday but he had no work to do and he persuaded the boy to take a half day. They headed out in the early afternoon and found an isolated place with a good view. They were there for hours. Lucas's husband told him that it was one of the happiest days of his life, a detail Lucas conveys with both shame and sympathy. That's what he and the boy were in the middle of, a happiest day, when they felt a rolling motion underneath them. Looking up they saw in the distance the city from which now a great cloud of dust was rising.

AMINA THE RESEARCH FELLOW who audited my class in the fall became a friend. Each time I see her on campus she says two things to me. She asks me how my heart is, always placing the palm of her hand on her heart as she says it. And she says that she knows I'm thinking of them. The "them" she is referring to are four people who used to live in a house on the edge of Harvard Yard. The house is still standing near one of the entrances to Harvard Yard close to what is now Harvard Square. We know the names of the four: Venus, Bilhah, Titus, and Juba, two women and two men. And we know they were enslaved by two presidents of Harvard in the eighteenth century. I think of them almost every time I enter Harvard Yard, which is almost daily, but only Amina knows this. When she places her hand on her heart, I place my hand on my heart. Those four among the dozens, among the countless.

NO FEWER THAN TWENTY people were enslaved by Abner Coltrane in North Carolina at the beginning of the Civil War. Some of the enslaved were related to each other, some like Andrew and Mary Ann Coltrane were married to each other, but most were unrelated. Family separation was the norm under slavery and kinship was precarious. According to a judicial charge in January 1861 in Asheboro, North Carolina, Abner Coltrane maltreated one of his bondsmen, Alfred Coltrane. The charge accused Abner of creating a public nuisance and described an ordeal for Alfred who for an unknown offense was whipped and beaten for three hours on a public street in "an unusual, cruel, inhuman, barbarous and shocking manner." We don't know what happened later that night when the numerous black Coltranes got back to their quarters. Perhaps Alfred's serious wounds were tended by the others. Possibly those who cared for him included Andrew and Mary Ann, the great-grandparents of John Coltrane.

———

A LOT OF THE suffering we will witness in life will be greater than ours. There's the question of what we can do to help and the different question of what to do when we can't help. Often one thinks of another's suffering: my dear friend you have so much life due you, how can this be happening? (I'm at Mass General waiting to see Emily.) For the sake of loyalty we keep in our minds the imagination of their private anguish. We cycle through all the emotions with them but often we also think—or behave as if we think—the abyss is remote for us. We believe that there will be sufficient warning so that we can either save ourselves or at least minimize the shock. We want to think we can avoid suddenness, we want to think that we can prepare ourselves for suddenness. Then the ground opens up. Life is not only more terrible than we know it is more terrible than we can know. If we were aware of the full extent of shipwrecks on the sea floor we would never set out in our boats.

The moment will come when the one facing the greatest suffering is me. I will have to understand that my suffering has no greater meaning. I will have to accept the fact of my own extinction, will have to understand that my appearance, my voice, my gait, my preferences, and my mannerisms not to mention the innumerable nebulous traits that constitute everything I think of as my self, will vanish and will vanish very soon. In a hundred years I will not only be dead but I will also be meaningfully gone, surviving only as rumor, only as a trace. And that oblivion comes through suffering, a terrible path to a terrible fate.

We are in the time now when we cannot think of those who were born in the early 1930s without thinking they are soon to die. So many of them have died already. By straightforward logic, in a decade from now all those born in the early 1940s will be doomed. Twenty years from now to have been born in the 1950s will be to belong to the generation that is dying off. The 1960s. The 1970s. The 1980s will be for someone else what the 1930s are for us now: the mark of imminent farewell. The generations go completely, the few long-lived holdouts don't hold out for much longer than the rest. Death's combine harvester is the most thorough of machines. And yet, for now, in this hospital waiting room, in my forties and full of worry about a friend in her sixties, my aliveness is as total as my extinction someday will be. I am as quietly incredulous as those young kamikaze pilots in the final months of the war, those young captains and lieutenants who, having to imagine the unimaginable, wrote final letters that were delivered after their deaths. Take care of Mother, she now has no one else but you. I am sorry to be leaving you at such a time. Forgive me for causing you sorrow in your twilight years. In the future you might come to understand that I have done my duty.

SHE STANDS UP FROM the sofa perhaps to go get a glass of water from the kitchen and at just that moment I enter the living room. I walk up to her and bring my face close to hers. Our arms hang at our sides. Love is stunned into silence. She runs her hand along the scar on my forearm. I rest my right cheek on her right cheek. Our faces are the same warm temperature and I remain there for almost a full minute. We remain there, standing with our cheeks touching, in contact but without pressure.

THE TERCENTENARY THEATER—not an actual theater but the array of trees which creates a green-roofed cathedral in the heart of campus in the warmer months—is irregularly criss-crossed by walking paths and bounded primarily by four buildings: Memorial Church, Widener Library, Sever Hall, and University Hall. The last of these was designed by Charles Bullfinch and completed in 1815. More than twenty-five years ago, well before my time here, an artwork was installed in the Tercentenary Theater by the artist David Ward. It was called *Canopy*. There is a poem of the same title by Seamus Heaney written to accompany Ward's work, there is a publication with guest essays and photographs of the installation, and there is a recording online of a lecture Ward gave about the project sometime after it had been made. The main element of *Canopy* was sound. Ward installed thirty burlap-covered battery-operated speakers onto the trunks of trees, many of them mature elms. The covered speakers, looking a little like wasps' nests, were placed well above human height. Ward spoke in his lecture of feeling that the invitation put him in the predicament of how to respond to the impressive setting without being "positioned" by it. His solution was to have an assortment of recorded human voices in sibilant chorus during dusk hours. His chosen text was *Invisible Cities*, fragments of which were read in various languages. These readings were supplemented with additional stories about place, stories meaningful and personal to the various readers so that for a few hours each day for two weeks in the early summer of 1994 *Canopy* transformed the center of campus into a magic wood.

The installation must have had some of the hypnotic multivocal power of Janet Cardiff's *Forty Part Motet* which also comprises voices shaping and making space. But what strikes me most lastingly about *Canopy* is a much more minor point namely Ward's unusual use in his lecture of the word "positioned." Ward said he found himself presented with two options: to be positioned in the sense of appearing to celebrate the institution or to be positioned by somehow seeming to critique it. He didn't want to be in either of those positions. His wish to refuse being positioned attracted me at first and I identified with his refusal. But after a while I saw things differently. Why would he not wish to seem to critique the institution? "Seeming to critique" he had said: to seem, to appear. I would like to be unconcerned with the appearance of critiquing the institution. Each place has a deeper history than any person in that place and this place in particular has a definite point of view on its history. For all his disavowal Ward in making *Canopy* was positioned by the setting: he did celebrate the institution. Venus, Bilhah, Titus, and Juba were positioned too by an institution that owes their memory more than a small commemorative plaque. Louis Agassiz, famed zoologist and leading champion of "scientific" racism, was positioned too by a celebratory plaque. There is no view from nowhere.

IN CLASS MY STUDENTS watch Abbas Kiarostami's *Through the Olive Trees*. The woman who plays Mrs. Shiva is listed in the credits as Zarifeh Shiva but I can't find any other film in which she's credited. This, added to the fact of her sharing her character's name, makes it easy to conflate actor and character. Mrs. Shiva seems to be in her forties or fifties and is beautiful in a simple and crushing way, the beauty of a woman seen on a street who is oblivious to the fires she sets in the hearts of passersby. Mrs. Shiva's eyes are large and lined with kohl. In the film she is a producer or showrunner and one thinks of her as capable, reliable, and serene. She is important in the film but she isn't one of the main protagonists. And yet she's the one to whom my mind returns, her memorable face, her steady mien, her understated and perfectly played role.

Through the Olive Trees was released in 1994 and is like many other films by Kiarostami simple and repetitive. Or rather it makes complex and intentional use of simplicity and repetition. At the beginning of the film is a scene at a girls' school in rural Northern Iran featuring a director, Mrs. Shiva, and a gaggle of girls. The director asks the girls questions about themselves: their names, where they live, what subject they are studying. Mrs. Shiva takes their answers down. Some kind of casting is going on. The director is interested in having one of the girls play a role in a film that he is making in the area. The fictional director's film, part of the making of which we see, is thus a film within the film by Kiarostami we are watching.

A lot of the screen time of *Through the Olive Trees* is spent on repeated takes of one particular scene. One of the girls from the school in her mid to late teens has been cast as a newlywed. A boy who is perhaps a bit older plays her husband. Through take after take they can't seem to get their lines or movements right. Specifically in the girl's case she doesn't seem to want to say her lines. It turns out there's history between her and the boy: he has an unrequited love for her. Her family has turned him down because he is illiterate but he still wishes to convince the girl of his love. This emotional turbulence makes it difficult for either to follow the director's simple directions. The director is patient perhaps because he knows he is working with nonprofessionals or perhaps because as Kiarostami's fictional stand-in he takes a secret pleasure in the farcical nature of the failures. The boy is supposed to say: I can't find my shoes. The girl is supposed to say: maybe they are downstairs. The boy is supposed to go down the stairs and say: I can't find them. But they can't get it right. Either he says his lines wrong or she doesn't respond with hers or he comes down the stairs before she has responded. The director and his long-suffering crew request them to repeat the simple scene over and over.

ACCORDING TO IRA PECK who visited him in 1948 Thelonious Monk lived in a small tenement flat. In the bedroom were an upright piano, a cot, a dresser, a chair, and photographs. A photograph of Sarah Vaughan near the cot, one of Ellington above the piano. Most memorable was the photo of Billie Holiday pasted next to a red bulb on the ceiling. The details sound like Monk's music: the photo on the ceiling, the red bulb. Poignant as his unexpected notes. Sharp. He liked to lie back and gaze at Billie's photo and this is perhaps why his performance of "I Don't Stand a Ghost of a Chance with You" recorded in 1957 sounds so much in its stuttering and heartbreak like the version she recorded two years earlier on

Music for Torching. Similar tune: Johannes Brahms only took one composition student, Gustav Jenner, whom he met late in 1887. Jenner's father, a physician, had committed suicide three years earlier after he had been found to have been abusing female patients. Perhaps the son for this reason was keen to adopt a father figure. Many years later in his 1930 memoir Jenner describes Brahms's apartment. In the living room was a desk and a piano and above the piano a medallion-portrait of Robert and Clara Schumann. The entrance to the apartment was through the bedroom and it was that Viennese interior design flaw that allowed Jenner a glimpse of Brahms's bedroom and the bed and over the bed the engraving of J. S. Bach.

LUCAS'S HUSBAND AND THE boy spring up in fright. They know what has happened. They have just seen a city destroyed before their eyes, the city in which nearly everyone the boy loves lives. They pack up their things. Lucas doesn't tell me that they have to get dressed first but that detail is implied. They get into the borrowed car and Lucas's husband drives like a madman all the way back to the city. Port-au-Prince is a shocking ruin. There are cries of agony from deep inside collapsed buildings. He brings the boy close to his neighborhood. What should he do? Darkness is falling. He barely knows this boy. He drops him off.

Lucas's husband's American colleagues are mostly accounted for but his Haitian colleagues are scattered to the four winds in search of family members. The following day he somehow reaches the boy by phone and finds out that the worst has happened: both parents dead, two of three brothers dead. (At this detail I feel bad for having thought of them as thugs.) Lucas's husband is crippled with guilt. He leaves some money in an envelope, not a small amount but still too small, and asks a junior staff member to deliver it to the boy. Undoubtedly the money isn't delivered. He doesn't see the boy before he leaves the country. He returns to Houston with that grief buried in him.

ON AUGUST 25 2012, the day Neil Armstrong died and *Voyager 1* entered interstellar space, the *Morgunblaðið* reported that a foreign tourist had gone missing at the volcanic canyon of Eldgjá. A group had disembarked to see the canyon and when they got back on the bus one woman wasn't there. There had been an all-day search and the tourist hadn't been found. The police bulletin described her as a woman of Asian descent in her twenties, dressed in dark clothing, a speaker of good English. She was carrying a small bag. The Stjarnan Rescue Squad from Skaftártunga had searched the area in cars and ATVs and had explored all the trails around the river. Additional forces had been called in from Rangárvalla and Vestur-Skaftafellssýsla.

The following day the *Morgunblaðið* reported that the massive search operation had continued until about 3:00 A.M. Only then was it realized that the woman had been found or, rather, that she had never been lost: she had been on the tour bus the entire time. Not only had she changed her clothes, leading to a confusion in the police description, but she herself had not recognized that the person being described was her. She had participated in the search for herself.

This was all more than seven years ago. Why did the story

resurface in the media late last year? Why had it only then become truly international with many news outlets reporting on it as though it had only just happened? It went viral and was seized on as a metaphor for those who wanted to point out political hypocrisies. A particularly popular one involved Justin Trudeau participating in a climate march: look, people said, Trudeau in a climate march is just like that woman who joined a search for herself. The Eldgjá incident became the only thing that social media recognized: an entertainment. Whatever could elicit laughter in it became the only thing that was legible in it. In none of the reports was the woman named. Not a woman, not a person, a funny incident.

MASSACHUSETTS IS SIMPLY HOME for Sadako. It was different for me and moving here altered my sense of what it meant to live with history. I had experienced New York City as a place tense with the nineteenth century. In Massachusetts I am aware of deeper time and older layers. New York was anciently settled too and the colonial encounter there no less bruising but Massachusetts somehow seems to present a more apparent vertical plunge into time. To be here is to be reminded of first principles, of who founded what and where they did it, of whose life was made impossible once the whites began to immigrate into this territory. This terrain is the morning of the new country, its first few pages. The historical record everywhere present in these towns immerses each day in a distant past, marks each place with the hard lines of the seventeenth century, the eighteenth century, the nineteenth century, the twentieth century, the twenty-first century.

The archives are full of voices. There was the letter sent in September 1753 by Samuel Moho, a resident of Stoughton, to William Shirley, governor of the Province of Massachusetts Bay. The petition comes from Moho and his fellow Ponkapoag Massachusett petitioners Abigail George, Samuel George, Hannah George, Dinah Moho, James Quok, and Sarah Moho. Their preamble is irradiated with the sorrow of dispossession. *Our woodlands have been plundered by many persons so that our cedar swamps and timber trees have been destroyed and our firewood cut off of our land.* The request in the letter is a simple one. They are dissatisfied with the military managers placed over them who are unjust. There have been harsh imprisonments and random cruelties. The petitioners wish for more humane rulers. But the sorrow in the letter extends to the self-abnegating tone they feel they must take in order to be heard. *We look upon you as our Fathers,* they write to the ones who are not their fathers. *We believe you love to be kind to us,* they write to those who do not love to be kind to them. *Do not be angry at our complaints.* The letter is attested by all, with those who cannot sign placing an "X" next to their names.

I'M IN THE GARAGE looking for a quick-release plate for my tripod. My left eye suddenly goes again. I had turned to face the light coming through the transparent panels on the upper part of the garage door. I felt pressure at the back of my eye. Then a gray curtain descended over my field of vision. There's no pain as there was no pain on previous occasions. I go into the living room to tell Sadako. I tell her I don't want her to worry. I don't know if she is worried or not. She suggests I go lie down in the bedroom and asks if I want a cold compress.

The first time it happened, nine years ago, it was on a morning after I had stayed up late finishing Virginia Woolf's diaries. Last night I read "The Death of a Moth." Will all the coincidences of our lives eventually be explained? Is there a cosmic ledger where it all adds up? Sadako asks if I am sure about the cold compress. I tell her I expect the gray to dissolve by itself. We are in the half dark of the bedroom. Now there's a definite flicker of worry on her face. She goes downstairs and when she comes back up a quarter of an hour later my vision is mostly restored. I am reading a book not resting my eyes.

EMILY'S WIG IS SIMILAR in color and cut to what her hair used to be, gray curls down to her earlobes. But I know she's been on chemo and can see that it's a wig. *I'm wearing a wig,* she says brightly. She also has on a dragonfly brooch which is unusual as she's not one to wear brooches. It's been hell, she says, and I hate that I'm saying what everyone says about chemo, that it's hell. There's supposed to be another round in two weeks. I don't know if I can go through with it. Anguish is really hard to talk about when people only expect you to talk about discomfort. You do feel like this bizarre outlier, undergoing your suffering while everyone else has their lives and their joys. Mariam says I must go through with it but I don't know if I must. Why must I? (Why must we go on living the fisherman said.)

I want to divert the conversation. I ask her how she's getting along with the aluminizing project in the Atacama but she just looks at me sadly. Astronomy too has been lost. But then she regains her voice. Life is months, she says. A tuft of time here, a tuft of time there, these months and months that flow into each other. It's changing all the time, she says, it's changing us in ways we don't even know. Somehow I see that it's this block of time for which there's no name, she says, not a year, not a week, not a single month. It is one group of months after another, though "group" also feels like the wrong word. A hundred days, two hundred days. I don't mean seasons, nothing so regular as that. But we are so in the thick of it that we don't remember the details. A cloud of months and then another cloud, a dwindling supply of clouds.

LUCAS IS TALKATIVE AND awkward. I feel great peace in his company. The third time we meet he says he knows I first befriended his father in Europe but he's not clear on the exact circumstances. It was in Basel in 1995, I say. Oh yes that makes sense, he says, my aunt Agnes lived there at the time. I was doing Eurail, I tell him, in late summer just before the beginning of my undergraduate year abroad in Göttingen. That Saturday at the Kunstmuseum in Basel was quiet maybe because it was so early. The museum has been enlarged now and it has an impressive modern wing. Back then there was a greater contrast between the stolid municipal-looking build- ing and the grandeur of some of the pieces in its collection. I did not at that time have much experience of European art yet and when I went through a museum I wasn't looking critically. But I was looking. I went from room to room in a state of awe. I tried to spend more time with the pictures than with the captions.

I did have at the time a particular interest in Hans Holbein
the Younger and the Kunstmuseum's collection was unusually rich in his works with good reason: Holbein had worked
in Basel as a young man before going on to the more complicated and more successful phase of his career at the court of
Henry VIII. That morning I saw Holbein's portraits of Eras-
mus of Rotterdam at a writing table, of Bonifacius Amer-
bach, and of his own wife, unflatteringly depicted with pallid
and blotchy skin, with their two oldest children. But the im-
pact of those skillful portraits was immediately cast in the
shade by his terrifying masterpiece *The Dead Christ in the
Tomb*. Just a foot high and nearly seven feet long, the panel
depicts Christ supine, life-size, and nearly naked. Far from
being an image of sacrificial love Holbein's painting is a stark
almost obscenely clinical depiction of the body of a dead
man, a dead man before he is a dead Christ. The body is ema-
ciated and rigid and there are grotesque discolorations at the
places where it has been pierced: the hand, the foot, between
the ribs. The brown hair on the figure's head is matted and
the necrotically gray face bears a look of surprise, the mouth
wide open, the eyes sunken, the same look one sees on the
faces of murdered dissidents, the same nightmarish look I remember seeing in press photos of the summarily executed
bandits the police used to parade in Lagos when I was a boy.
The only concession to decorum in Holbein's painting is a
white loincloth. That morning in Basel I did not yet know
that it was this very painting that caused such a crisis of faith
for Prince Myshkin in Dostoevsky's *The Idiot*.

But in a museum life floods the viewer in waves. No mood
remains unchanged. After *The Dead Christ in the Tomb* there

were altarpieces, flower arrangements, landscapes. And I became aware as I moved from room to room that there was a
man who arrived in each room just after me or was already
there when I entered. We had not yet made eye contact but it
was inevitable that we would eventually find ourselves standing in front of the same painting. When we did we stood
there for a little longer than we ordinarily might have, detained not so much by the painting itself as by the awareness
of viewing it with another. He was the one who spoke. The
way that glass is placed so close to the edge, he said, anything
can happen. Life can be smashed in an instant. That's what
makes this a vanitas piece.

He was older than me. (How vivid now is my memory of
his face as I describe the day to Lucas.) The painting was titled *Still Life with Wineglass and Cut Lemon* and was by a
Dutch artist whose name I was encountering for the first
time, Jan Jansz van de Velde III. The panel was a field of
darkness, an arrangement in black and gray: dark roemer
glass, dark metalwork stem, dark tablecloth, stormy dark
background, the gloom of the panel enlivened mainly by the
half lemon and its depending yellow-and-white peel. Light
came in through a high window in the museum and created a
pale quadrilateral on the wall opposite the van de Velde painting. The man had made an invitation, which I took. We
looked at the next picture together and the one after that. We
spoke while looking at some paintings and some commanded
us to be silent. We moved through the galleries in sync:
Böcklin's *Island of the Dead*, the *Injured Jockey* by Degas, a
procession of Hodlers. The museum was busier now and the
presence of others made it easier for us to be a pair. In front

of Sophie Taeuber-Arp I told him my name and he told me his. There was a fine Cy Twombly and a sculpture by Giacometti.

A month later a letter arrived at the Global Exchange Program at the University of Göttingen. It had been sent from Chicago. That letter inaugurated the most voluminous and intense correspondence of my life. To begin with we wrote to each other twice a month. This went on for many years until email became easier. Then the pace became even more frequent. It was the great conversation. We wrote to each other of ordinary things and of immortal things, of art, music, literature, and memory. And we wrote to each other of death. In retrospect it feels mythic but at the time it was simply the texture of life. We had almost twenty years of this conversation with only two or three quiet stretches in the midst of it, never more than a few months. It slowed down only at the very end. Three and a half years without him now and I'm still at a loss.

IN THE COURSE OF my ordinary life in this ordinary winter I have a good sense of what tomorrow will look like. Predicting the day after tomorrow is only a bit less clear. From the point of view of today each successive tomorrow gets more obscured until one imagines the far future in which almost nothing can be seen at all and very little can be accurately guessed. The future is a series of ever less clear tomorrows. And yet one plans. In late March I'll finally make the trip to Santiago. I continue to work on the drafts of that lecture. In April Sadako and I will return to Japan for ten days. I will work on "Search Party" in Tokyo and we will visit her family in Osaka. In July I look forward to my first trip to Dakar and to the exhibition there. No decision made yet on the invitation to Hamburg or the possible exhibition in Huntsville. And in the midst of all that there's teaching and photography and writing.

The work I do takes me to places where I am received as a guest of honor, places where I try to think and speak and where I try to avoid speechifying. All of this is true but none of it is where reality is. There is another reality, the personal one. And then there's the secret one that is as dark as the blood beating in my veins, a cold river flowing undetected far from view, a place of uncertainty and premonition. Something is moving there that does not need me for its movement and that is taking me where I cannot imagine. A darkness to which the eyes can never become adjusted.

IT WON'T BE LONG now, maybe a matter of weeks, when I will pick up my mail from the department and there will be a white envelope with black trim. On the inside will be the card that says: *Emily Tamara Brown, Shoemaker Professor of Astronomy*. I cannot exempt my friend from the final blow. Afterwards there will be the memorial service in Jamaica Plain, the clack of heels on the stone slabs of the floor of a church in winter. We will embrace Mariam and her children and console her with our useless words, a sad finality on which I brood as though it has already come to pass.

THE WHEELS ON THE bus go round and round. There was the merchant John Codman, famous for his cruelty, who kept many people enslaved among them a man named Mark and a woman named Phillis. Not least of Codman's crimes was the separation of Mark from his family. But Mark was literate and he read the whole Bible to find out if he could kill Codman without incurring blood guilt. We don't know what he found. It doesn't matter. What we know is that Mark could not suppress the need to do what he had to do. In league with Phillis and others he obtained some arsenic and they found a way to give their master seven small doses of it with his meals and Codman sickened and died in July 1755. But then the plot was uncovered and three justices, all of them Harvard alumni, condemned Mark and Phillis to death and shipped their co-conspirators off to Caribbean sugar plantations.

Avon Hill where my studio is was once called Gallows Hill. Many of the houses here are still grand but many have been converted into multifamily condos. At the end of the block is a knoll and on this knoll Phillis was in September 1755 tied to a stake and set on fire, an extremely rare punishment in colonial New England, an act of terrifying cruelty. Ten yards away Mark was hanged. His body was transferred to a gibbet in Charlestown and chained to it for public viewing. A visitor three years later remarked the unusual state of the body's preservation. Twenty years later Mark's body was still there on display in the open in Charlestown as an example to others, his bones gradually whitening in the sun. I have not always wished to be the killing kind. The wheels on the bus go round and round. But now I'll be the killing kind. I'll make kin with those whose servitude cannot be trusted, those who have little chance of growing old.

———

I FEEL SURE I have seen the man before. I must have had a conversation with him somewhere but my memory fails me. He is slender and tall and very dark-skinned. I think he must be Senegalese and just as I form that thought I realize who he is. He's the man I had a run-in with outside the Louvre. But now he's smiling broadly, he's all sweetness, and he's offering me something: a clasped leather bag the size of a small sack. I tell him I'm not interested. He keeps smiling and extending the bag towards me. *Ouvrez-le,* he says. *Ouvrez-le.* And then he says in English: you really have no idea what it's like. He eventually wears me down and he's practically laughing as I reach for the clasp and open the bag. It's dark inside and my heart pounds. I lean forward for a better look. The bag contains an enormous writhing lizard.

I HAVE OTHER FRIENDS who share my love of the Cello Suites but it was he who introduced me to Anner Bylsma's version. Anything that connected to the Cello Suites thereafter was something I wanted to share with him. There are too many fine readings of the Suites to count and the works represent such a clear statement of technical skill and ambition that cellists will always strive to add their own interpretations to the discography. But when Bylsma died last year I couldn't discuss it with my friend. When I discovered and became enraptured by a recording of the suites by Arnau Tomàs I couldn't discuss it with my friend. Nothing can be new anymore for my friend. The great conversation has become a monologue.

———

SHE'S COMING DOWN THE stairs as I'm going up. She's wearing a thin shirt. My left hand brushes her left hand. She turns around and takes my hand in hers. Between her thumb and four fingers I place my four fingers. Between my thumb and four fingers her four fingers are placed and we slowly walk up the stairs. Not for a moment longer can I bear not to be inside her.

THROUGH THE OLIVE TREES takes place in a devastated landscape. The girls' school was only recently rebuilt and the set of the film within a film is a ruin. An earthquake had struck the area in 1990 killing between 35,000 and 50,000 people. The enormity of this disaster remains in the background of *Through the Olive Trees*. The minor comedy of love, the minor tragedy of love, is center stage. Meanwhile rural people go on with their lives, repairing roads, fetching water, playing parts for a visiting director. The boy says maybe it was God's will that the girl's parents died in the earthquake since they had rejected his proposal. But her grandmother who is now responsible for her holds the line and continues to refuse the boy. His callousness takes on a different tone when we understand that almost all of his own family was wiped out too. And for the newlyweds that the boy and the girl are playing there's a similarly pervasive experience of bereavement. Sixty-five of the fictional young husband's relatives were killed.

No dead bodies are shown, there are no flashbacks, and little is said directly about this mass death. What we see is the strange calm of an aftermath. We see people who have come through the impossible and have resigned themselves to the necessity of being practical. Survival is living on, living above the wreckage: *survivre, supervivencia*. You think you know how hard life can get. Then something else happens, something of a kind different to what you ever allowed yourself to expect and you have to revise your whole picture. This doesn't stop happening, there is no end of surprise. Strangeness arrives again and again, without end. We live on the accumulated ruins of experience. *Überleben, sopravvivere*. In the film the landscape is what carries most of that grief across to us. The cinematography rests on the view and little further explanation is required. The olive groves, the mountains, the ordinariness of workers and migrants in an impoverished area, the mutual bemusement of visitors from the city and survivors in the countryside: all of that is left to speak for itself as though without adjectives.

I'LL BUY THE FLOWERS myself. He has many other things to do at home. He'll trim dead leaves off the houseplants, fill the ice trays, bring in the bottles of red wine from the garage. He wants to sort through the pile of unopened mail: insurance, WGBH, the Gardner, West Elm, credit card offers. For the second year there's a misdelivered New Year's card meant for the other Ellis Street in the other Cambridge. He'll handwrite a note and send it on its way. It's a bright crisp morning, so cold it takes one's breath away. The front gravel is covered in glitterfrost.

I return in the late morning. While he's oiling my hair upstairs he tells me that he heard from Emily. The news three weeks ago was grim and we feared the worst but there now seems to have been a dramatic remission. The doctors are as surprised as Emily herself is. Things are still uncertain—it will be years before there's any certainty—but it seems as if she's caught a rare lucky break. The second round of chemo was effective, he tells me, and she expects to be back teaching in the fall. While he's saying all this I begin softly to weep. It is the reprieve that brings me to tears and now he comforts me as I comforted him when he, weeping, had first told me she was dying.

And this news recharges our day, brings a lightness to it. The hours of preparation for the party fly by. In the middle of the afternoon I have to take a quick work call as Finn has some irregular numbers he wants to discuss. Tunde returns from his studio at five and we set to the cooking. Tonight it is to be gumbo in two large batches, one with smoky andouille sausages, the other for vegetarians. In the darkness our guests will begin arriving, boots off at the door, coats on the bed in my study upstairs. For a brief moment each guest is in the silence of a room in someone else's home, divesting themselves of unneeded warmth. They can hear music from unseen speakers: Gladys Knight's "Since I Fell for You." Their eyes rest on my botanical drawings and on the framed photograph of John Coltrane. Then they come down into the hubbub.

Tunde is making aviation cocktails with Sean's help and the guests are drinking them as fast as they are being made. Each coupe has violet petals in it. Tunde and Sean can't keep up with demand and finally give up and nudge the party towards red wine. Masako is deep in conversation with Lucas and his husband, Jarvis, neither of whom I have met before. Jarvis is short, gray-haired, and strikingly handsome. Their children are upstairs in the guest room absorbed in their iPads. Taiwo is laughing with Tunde's friend Amina. Rae and their partner run up to the roof deck for a smoke. All this delightful activity and liveliness. The doorbell rings and it's Anthony whom we haven't seen since either his Pulitzer nomination or his divorce. He is with a woman I don't know. We roll his wheelchair in. Behind is my friend and colleague Angela. Clusters of other people, some of whom I am less familiar with including a couple of other research fellows Amina has brought with her. The dining room table lit up by a great vase of peonies, delphiniums, and hydrangeas. Real flowers, false season. Angela is telling us about her participation in the revival of spoken Wampanoag. Someone changes the music. "Cranes in the Sky." Frank Ocean's "Nights." Bowls are passed around with heaps of white rice on which the gumbo is served and it's as though people don't realize how hungry they are until they began to eat. Drinks are expected at parties but real food isn't. But we love to feed people. What a gift to get to do this in community. How great is what surrounds us, how insubstantial what preoccupies us. I make eye contact with my love, the one who keeps me from losing my head, the one I keep from losing his footing.

In the lees of the party Rae brings out a small bag and out of the bag a recorder. They begin to play it and a hush falls over the room. They are standing in front of the cabinet on which the wooden ci wara we bought in Wells is displayed. Lucas's children tiptoe downstairs and peer around the stairwell. I can't tell if Rae is improvising or if they are playing a set tune but the playing is focused, natural, elegiac, with sustained notes. They seem to be playing in Phrygian mode and in one section there are ostinato figures that sound Andalusian or like a muezzin's call. Then the tune finds its way to a beautiful melody that is so disguised and unexpected that it takes me a moment to identify it. "Naima."

I imagine this party as seen from the street: the faces of people who are listening to live music, the warm color of these lights. Then the street as seen from the party: cold and crisp and dark. Snow has been absent all month. It was thought there would finally be some tonight. But no, no snow, just the temperature dropping.

THE PLEASURE OF HAVING the house full of people is exceeded perhaps only by the pleasure of seeing the last few leave. My sister helps start the cleanup and then goes to bed. The bulk of it can wait until morning. I tell Sadako that I'm going for a walk with my camera. I expect I'll be back in about twenty minutes. I had shown her my daytime photograph of the hedge because she can identify plants. It wasn't jasmine, as I'd thought, it was honeysuckle. The night is clear, the air is icy, and breathing is a challenge. I am warmly dressed. I set up my tripod before leaving the house and when I get to the hedge—it is evergreen but its flowers are long gone—I am able to put myself in position quickly. It is late, past 2:00 A.M., and I have no nerves this time, no worry. Accustomed by now to the air I breathe deeply and evenly as I bend over and look into the viewfinder. The hedge, distinctly unruly on an otherwise tame street, is partly lit by a streetlamp. My first shot is a fifteen-second exposure that results in a photograph that is too bright. A second photograph at eight seconds is too inky. I experiment and finally settle on eleven seconds. I move the tripod back a few feet, refocus, press the shutter. But now the frame is too wide. The original closeness was the right distance but I feel I am not including enough of the house behind the hedge. Those windows are important. The threat of "private property," the memory of that threat, is part of the desired image. I swivel the camera a bit to the right, refocus, and press the shutter. Then increasing the ISO and reducing the shutter speed and keeping the aperture at f/8 I make one last image.

My fingers are starting to go numb in spite of the gloves I have on. But I feel no sense of hurry. The glossy leaves of the honeysuckle are perfectly still in the frigid air and innumerable. The vastness of the night is all around me, the leaves are darkest green. I look up. The starry sky is a glinting sea. There's Saturn, there's Arcturus, on this January night. The spectacle of Mark's body out there in the cold year on year, a terrifying fate but only to the living. The number of gods in the Yoruba pantheon is as many as you can think of, plus one more.

WHEN I COME BACK in I take a hot shower. The evening's interactions glimmer in my mind like a cloud of distant lights. It feels good to be warmed up but as I get into bed I have an attack of vertigo. It has never happened to me before but I recognize it. I know it from how my mother has spoken of hers. When she describes it she moves her hand from side to side to describe how the room seems to be moving. I also know it from accounts I have read in books. I am doubly disoriented: the room does seem to pitch and spin but I am perplexed as well by the sudden frailty of finding myself experiencing something I have only heard described. On the bed I try to be still but the room continues to move. My head vibrates like a struck bell and I experience a surge of nausea. While all this is happening I'm describing it to Sadako. I tell her it's strange how accurate all the descriptions by other people have been. My mind races ahead. I might have an underlying illness, this might be something that will happen many times from now on. This might be nothing or it might be something else. Uneasy minutes pass. Then the vertigo subsides and I begin to drift off.

SHE PLACES HER HAND on my fist. Her hand covers my fist. I let my hand fall open. She moves her hand down and crosses her wrist against mine and now I'm almost asleep. When and where were you happiest? My one remaining contact with wakefulness is the flat inside of her wrist resting on the flat inside of mine, as though each wrist were seeking the other's pulse. I listen for the soft beat of blood through the skin. I listen as best as I can in the dimming stillness. I slow my breathing and soon I hear nothing.

TEJU COLE was born in the United States in 1975 to Nigerian parents and grew up in Lagos. His books include the novel *Open City*, the essay collections *Known and Strange Things* and *Black Paper*, and the experimental photo book *Blind Spot*. He has been honored with the PEN/Hemingway Award, the Internationaler Literaturpreis, the Windham-Campbell Prize, and a Guggenheim Fellowship, among others. He is an elected member of the American Academy of Arts and Sciences. Cole is currently a professor of the practice of creative writing at Harvard University and a contributing writer to *The New York Times Magazine*.

tejucole.com

Instagram: @_tejucole

ABOUT THE TYPE

This book was set in Fournier, a typeface named for
Pierre-Simon Fournier (1712–68), the youngest son
of a French printing family. He started out engraving
woodblocks and large capitals, then moved on to fonts
of type. In 1736 he began his own foundry and made
several important contributions in the field of type
design; he is said to have cut 147 alphabets of his own
creation. Fournier is probably best remembered as
the designer of St. Augustine Ordinaire, a face that
served as the model for the Monotype Corporation's
Fournier, which was released in 1925.